'Joseph was huddled under the bedclothes. Estelle sat on his bed.

"What's wrong, Joe?"

"Nothing." His voice was muffled.

"Is it about the concert?"

Joseph didn't answer. But Estelle knew it *was*. She didn't see how he could get out of it now. She pictured Mum and Dad, and lots of friends and relations, and *Grandmother,* all sitting in the hall on Saturday, all watching Joseph . . .'

Estelle's small brother, Joseph, is scared stiff at the thought of acting in the school play! He especially wants to do well because Grandmother, who has come all the way from Africa on a visit, will be there to see him. Estelle wants to help Joseph. But what can she do?

Also available by Marjorie Newman,
and published by Young Corgi Books:

THE AMAZING PET
THE SCARY MOUSE

GREEN MONSTER MAGIC is one of a series of
books, BY MYSELF BOOKS, which are specially
selected to be suitable for beginner readers.

GREEN MONSTER MAGIC

MARJORIE NEWMAN

ILLUSTRATED BY PAT LUDLOW

YOUNG CORGI BOOKS

GREEN MONSTER MAGIC

A YOUNG CORGI BOOK o 552 526207

Originally published in Great Britain by
Hodder and Stoughton Children's Books

PRINTING HISTORY
Hodder and Stoughton edition published 1988
Young Corgi edition published 1990

Text copyright © Marjorie Newman 1988
Illustrations copyright © Pat Ludlow 1990

This book is set in 18/24pt Garamond by
Kestrel Data, Exeter

Young Corgi Books are published by Transworld Publishers Ltd., 61-63
Uxbridge Road, Ealing, London W5 5SA, in Australia by Transworld
Publishers (Australia) Pty. Ltd., 15-23 Helles Avenue, Moorebank,
NSW 2170, and in New Zealand by Transworld Publishers (N.Z.) Ltd.,
Cnr. Moselle and Waipareira Avenues, Henderson, Auckland.

Made and printed in Great Britain by
Cox & Wyman Ltd., Reading, Berks.

GREEN MONSTER MAGIC

1 *Stage Fright*

Estelle sat on the floor of the
school hall and went hot all over.
It was Thursday evening. The
Squirrel Club were having their
meeting in the school, as usual.
Usually, the Squirrel Club was

fun. Everyone collected things. They helped each other with their collections. And they often went on club expeditions to see other collections or to get more things for their own.

But this wasn't their usual kind of meeting. They were having their last practice before the club's concert on Saturday. And Estelle's six-year-old brother Joseph was up on the stage.

Because it was the last practice, all the children were being allowed to watch each other. Joseph's group was doing a space play. And he was being *useless*. Estelle couldn't *bear* it for him.

He was captain of the space-ship. She'd helped him remember

his words. And she'd watched some of his other practices. Sometimes he'd been really good.

But whenever he'd made a mistake, he'd looked as if he

wanted to curl up and die. And she'd wanted to curl up and die as well.

Tonight, he was making more mistakes than he'd ever done before. And he didn't sound a bit like the captain of a spaceship.

'Um . . . Aliens in sight . . . um . . . they could be enemy aliens . . . um . . . Crew . . . Stand by . . .'

His voice stopped. Margaret,

the club leader, said, 'Come on, Joseph! You can do better than that! Try it just once more, dear!'

Joseph took a deep breath. He stepped forward – and his captain's hat came down over his eyes.

The watching children laughed so much, they rocked backwards and forwards.

But Estelle didn't laugh. Nor did Joseph.

Nor did Margaret. She hurried across to Joseph, and took the hat off for him. Then she clapped her hands for silence.

'I'm ashamed of you all!' she said. 'How do you expect Joseph to do his best, with such sillies in the audience? This is the dress-rehearsal, when we let you dress

up specially to find out if the costumes are all right. Joseph's hat needs some padding, that's all. His suit looks absolutely splendid!'

Joseph was wearing a white suit with gold buttons. He did look splendid. But it was no good. After his hat came down over his eyes, his acting was worse than ever.

Estelle heard one of the boys muttering names under his breath. Names that black children were sometimes called. Estelle felt upset. But she didn't let anyone see. Mum and Dad said it was best to take no notice of people who were stupid enough to call other people names.

Margaret didn't grumble at Joseph. But as soon as his play was over, Estelle saw him rush out to go to the loo. She hoped he wasn't crying out there . . .

'Eight-year-olds! I want you to practise your dance once more!' called Margaret. So Estelle

couldn't go after him. She climbed up on to the stage.

As soon as the music started she forgot about Joseph and everything else. She loved dancing.

'That was much better!' cried Margaret, at the end. 'Remember to curtsy and bow! Well done!'

Grinning, they jumped down off the stage. Joseph had come back, and was sitting by himself. Estelle went to sit with him. He got up and moved away. She let him go.

'Children!' Margaret clapped her hands again. 'Listen! We've finished now. Take your costumes off *very* carefully, and give them to one of the helpers. Remember to be here at half past one on Saturday, in Classroom

One, to get ready. And children – thank you all very much for helping to put on the concert. We ought to earn enough money to keep the club going for another year!'

The children cheered. One reason why Mum and Dad wanted Joseph and Estelle to be in the concert was that if you wanted to belong to the club it was only fair to help get the money to pay for it. Another reason was they thought it would be fun. But the *big* reason was that Grandmother would be there!

Grandmother still lived in Nigeria, in Africa. But she was coming on a visit. And she was arriving tomorrow!

It was very exciting. Estelle couldn't *wait* to see Grand-mother!

If only Joseph had been OK as the captain . . .

Mum had come to meet them.

'Well – how was the practice?' she asked.

'OK,' said Joseph. Estelle
sighed. Joseph was afraid he
would get into trouble if Mum
and Dad knew how badly things
went at his practices.

When they got home, Dad was
out. He was a doctor. He often
had to go out unexpectedly on an

emergency call if people were suddenly taken ill.

Estelle and Joseph had supper. Then Mum said, 'Off to bed, you two! We have to be up early in the morning to get to the airport!'

Estelle hopped and danced up the stairs. She and Joseph had

been given a day off school to go and meet Grandmother. It was great . . .

But when Estelle was in bed, she heard Joseph crying softly.

After a moment, she got up, and crept across to his room.

2 Grandmother

Joseph was huddled under the
bedclothes. Estelle sat on his bed.

'What's wrong, Joe?'

'Nothing.' His voice was
muffled.

'Is it about the concert?'

Joseph didn't answer. But Estelle knew it *was*. She sighed. She didn't see how he could get out of it now. She pictured Mum and Dad, and lots of friends and relations, and *Grandmother*, all sitting in the hall on Saturday, all watching Joseph . . . She shivered. Joseph went on crying.

'Look,' she said, 'I'll think of something.'

'What?' asked Joseph.

'I don't know yet!' Estelle sounded cross because she was worried. Mum called up the stairs:

'Estelle! Are you in Joe's room?'

Estelle shot back to her own bed. 'No!' she called. 'I'm in my own.'

'Go to sleep!' called Mum. 'Tomorrow's a busy day!'

Estelle lay down. But it was hard to get to sleep. Some of the time she thought about meeting Grandmother. And some of the time she thought about Joseph . . . She fell asleep at last.

Next morning, none of them wanted much breakfast. Mum and Dad were as excited as Estelle. Even Joseph cheered up. Dressed in their best clothes, they

all got into Dad's car and set out
for the airport.

The airport was hot and
crowded. The plane was late.
But at *last* it arrived. Presently,
Grandmother came walking in

with the rest of the passengers. Estelle knew at once which one was Grandmother. Grandmother looked exactly like the photographs Mum had of her.

For one second Estelle felt shy. Then they were all hugging each other, and laughing, and all trying to talk at once.

Grandmother said she didn't feel a *bit* tired. She'd managed to sleep on the plane. On the way back in the car she liked everything they showed her. And she liked their house. And she liked her room. And she liked the meal Mum hurried to set out!

And she loved it when friends and relations began to arrive, to help with the celebration. She put on a gorgeous Nigerian costume, full of bright colours. And she wore a splendid head-dress.

Everyone was hungry now! Estelle helped to set out plenty of dishes. They had a feast!

They had jollof rice with peppered chicken, groundnut

stew, sauces, sweet potato, plan-
tain, pineapple, mango fruit, and
oranges you could eat the
Nigerian way – by cutting off the
top, then holding the orange with
both hands and sucking out the
juice . . .

And there were other foods,
and wine, and fizzy drinks.

And there was lots of music and
dancing.

It was great!

They gave presents to Grandmother, and she gave presents to

them. For Estelle there were glass bangles. They'd been made in Africa. The way they were made was secret, Grandmother told her. Only people in one little part of Africa knew how to make them.

Estelle wore her bangles proudly.

Grandmother told them about her journey to England, starting with a ride along the expressway – a fast road – to Lagos. And she told them about Lagos.

And then – in the middle of all the happiness – Mum said, 'Grandmother, tomorrow you'll be able to see Estelle and Joseph in a concert at their club!'

Grandmother smiled. 'I *will* look forward to that!'

But five minutes later, Estelle found Joseph up in his bedroom, hiding under his bed.

'I'm never coming out!' he said.

3 Green Monster

'Don't be stupid, Joe!' cried
Estelle. 'You can't stay there for
ever! Specially not with all the
visitors we've got! They'll find
you!'

'I shan't come out,' said Joe,

and turned his back to her.

Estelle went downstairs, twisting her hands together because she was so worried. At the bottom of the stairs she met Mrs Johnson. Mrs Johnson lived next door. She was probably about as old as Grandmother, but she was one of Estelle's special friends. She'd come in to meet Grandmother. Now, she said, 'Estelle, what's wrong? You look as happy as a chicken in a thunderstorm!'

Estelle smiled a little. Then she sighed. Mrs Johnson said, 'Come on! You can tell *me*! Let's go over to my house, where it's quiet.'

Two minutes later, Estelle was sitting in one armchair, with Mrs Johnson in another. And two

minutes after *that*, Mrs Johnson knew what Estelle was worrying about.

For a moment, Mrs Johnson sat and thought. Then she said, 'Estelle, I'm going to tell you a story.'

Tell a story! Right now, when Estelle was upset about Joseph, *and* was supposed to be at Grandmother's celebration?

Then Mrs Johnson began, with the words Estelle loved:

'A story, a story. Let it come,

let it go.' And Estelle forgot everything else while she listened.

'Once,' said Mrs Johnson, 'there was a monkey who wanted to get across a stream. Lying on the bank was a crocodile, so big, so big, so big. The crocodile said, "Monkey, I'll take you across this stream! Get on my back!" The monkey thought hard, because crocodiles have many teeth, and mouths so big, so big, so big. But there was no other way. So the

monkey climbed on to the crocodile's back.'

Estelle held her breath. Mrs
Johnson went on:

'The crocodile started out
across the stream. But right in the
middle, he stopped. "Now," he
said, "I must kill you!"

'The monkey began to shiver
and shake. "Why must you kill
me? I'm not good to eat!" he
cried.

' "I must kill you because my

wife is very ill," said the crocodile. "The only medicine to make
her well is a monkey's heart. I
must give her your heart to
swallow."

' "Wait!" cried the monkey. He thought very fast. "Listen!" he said. "My heart is small, so small, so small, so small! It won't be any use for a large creature like a crocodile! If you take me over the stream, I will run and fetch you *two* monkeys' hearts!"

'The crocodile thought hard,' Mrs Johnson went on, 'and in the end he agreed. He took the monkey safely to the other side. The monkey ran off into the forest.'

'And didn't come back!' cried Estelle.

'Oh, yes, he did!' smiled Mrs Johnson. 'And in his paw he held two funny little things which he gave to the crocodile. The crocodile's wife swallowed the two little things – and got well, so fast, so fast, so fast! But those little things weren't monkeys' hearts at all. They were dates.'

Estelle sat and thought. Then she said, 'The crocodile's wife got better because she *believed* they were monkeys' hearts, and would make her well.'

'Right,' nodded Mrs Johnson. She went over to her cabinet,

opened the door, and got out a little green monster, about six centimetres from nose to tail. 'This,' she said, with a twinkle in her eye, 'this may be magic! *Maybe* he has a secret for you – and for Joseph. Take him. He's yours.'

Puzzled, Estelle took the monster. 'Thank you,' she said.

'Now – back to the party!' cried Mrs Johnson.

The celebration was going well. No one had missed them.

But Dad had found Joseph, and made him come downstairs. Joseph looked unhappy.

Estelle peeped at the monster in her hand. She thought about the crocodile story. And she had an idea . . . But would it work?

4 *Magic Powers*

At half past one next day, Mum took Joseph and Estelle along to the school. Joseph was a funny, grey colour.

'Now don't you worry!' Mum told him. 'You're going to be great!'

Estelle held the green monster in her hand, and hoped her idea *would* work . . .

When they were both in their costumes, and Mum had gone over to sit in the hall, Estelle wriggled her way amongst the other children until she got to Joseph.

'Look!' she said. She showed him the monster. 'This monster has magic powers!'

Joseph didn't believe her. She *had* to make him believe it.

She spoke slowly.

'Anyone who holds this monster can do everything much better than usual. And I can *prove* it.' She put the monster down. Then she jumped, fairly high.

'See? That's how high I can jump *without* the monster. *Now* watch.'

She picked the monster up, and gave a huge jump.

'See?' she gasped. '*Much* higher.'

Joseph was listening . . . She said, 'A person who held this monster while they were acting would be able to *act* much better than usual . . . And if you like, I'll lend him to you.'

Joseph nodded eagerly. At that

moment, Margaret clapped her hands and·called, 'Children! Line up for the opening song!'

Estelle pushed the monster into Joseph's hand. Then she dived over to her own place in the line. Perhaps, *after* the concert, she'd tell him the crocodile story . . .

The opening song went splendidly. Estelle and Joseph saw Mum, and Dad, and Mrs Johnson, and Grandmother, and lots of friends and relations, all sitting in the hall, clapping and

clapping. Everyone was smiling
and happy. Estelle saw Joseph
smile, too.

Her dance went splendidly.
Everything was going splendidly.

Then came the space play.
Estelle could hardly bear it – but

she had to watch. She stood at the side of the stage, hidden by the curtains.

On came Joseph and his crew. Joseph's hand was closed tight round the green monster . . .

The audience gave them a clap to start them off.

And Joseph was splendid! He got all his words right. He moved at the right times. He sounded like a captain. And Margaret had padded his hat so that it stayed on properly.

At the end, the audience gave him a special clap. Mum and Dad and Grandmother looked very proud. Mrs Johnson was smiling all over her face.

The curtains swished together. Joseph turned round and saw Estelle. He was smiling all over *his* face, too.

'Joe,' said Estelle, 'can I have my monster back?'

Thoughtfully, she put it into her pocket.

Because maybe . . . just *maybe* . . . it *was* magic after all . . .

THE END

THE AMAZING PET

by Marjorie Newman

Everyone in Robert's family is amazingly good at something – except Robert. And he's fed up with being ordinary. But then he has a thought. He will have a pet. Nothing ordinary like a cat or dog. No, Robert is determined to have an *amazing* pet – and what could be more amazing than a giraffe? He's never heard of anyone having a giraffe for a pet before!

But what will Mum and Dad say when Robert's giraffe, George, comes home? Will they like him as much as he does? Perhaps he should keep it all a secret until everything is ready . . .

SBN 0 552 52469 7

THE SCARY MOUSE

by Marjorie Newman

Paul's friend Annette adores her new pet – a tiny white mouse with pretty brown markings, little pink ears and a long pink tail. She names her Fudge and takes the mouse *everywhere* with her.

Then Annette has an accident. Paul promises her that he will look after Fudge for her. But how can he? For Paul is frightened of the little mouse, frightened of her teeth, frightened that she might escape and run all over him . . .

SBN 0 552 525588

PURR

by Jennifer Zabel

'URGENT!' said the notice. 'Kitten needs home by Friday. Going to Cat Sanctuary if not taken.'

Katy, Nick and their baby brother Ben are determined to have a kitten – even though Dad hates cats! And how can Mum not help when they see the sad little sign in the pet shop?

But once the small tabby kitten arrives home, the children realize that they have a new problem. For not only does the naughty little kitten appear to do its best to upset Dad, but it also seems to be rather lonely. Maybe they now need a second kitten to keep him company . . .

SBN 0 552 525456

If you would like to receive a Newsletter about our new Children's books, just fill in the coupon below with your name and address (or copy it onto a separate piece of paper if you don't want to spoil your book) and send it to:

The Children's Books Editor
Transworld Publishers Ltd.
61–63 Uxbridge Road,
Ealing
London W5 5SA

Please send me a Children's Newsletter:

Name: ....

Address: ....

....

....

All Children's Books are available at your bookshop or newsagent, or can be ordered from the following address:
Transworld Publishers Ltd.
Cash Sales Department,
P.O. Box 11, Falmouth, Cornwall TR10 9EN

Please send a cheque or postal order (no currency) and allow 60p for postage and packing for the first book plus 25p for the second book and 15p for each additional book ordered up to a maximum charge of £1.90 in UK.

B.F.P.O. customers please allow 60p for the first book, 25p for the second book plus 15p per copy for the next 7 books, thereafter 9p per book.

Overseas customers, including Eire, please allow £1.25 for postage and packing for the first book, 75p for the second book, and 28p for each subsequent title ordered.

DUNCAN VERSUS the GOOGLEYS

KATE MILNER is a writer and illustrator based in Bedfordshire with her husband and son. In her career she has painted pub signs and made prints, been a teacher and a carer. When working at her local library, she fell in love with children's books and went on to become an illustrator, winning the Klaus Fugge Award for her picture book *My Name is Not Refugee*. *Duncan Versus the Googleys* is her first novel.

Pushkin Children's

DUNCAN VERSUS the GOOGLEYS

Kate Milner

Pushkin Press
71–75 Shelton Street
London wc2h 9jq

Duncan Versus the Googleys was first published by Pushkin Press in 2020

1 3 5 7 9 8 6 4 2

ISBN 13: 978-1-78269-251-5

Designed and typeset by Tetragon, London
Printed and bound by CPI Group (UK) Ltd, Croydon, cro 4yy

www.pushkinpress.com

He laid a clean piece of newspaper on the table, lit a candle in a jam jar and arranged two chocolate biscuits and a grape on each plate.

- I -

THREE BIRTHDAY PRESENTS
AND A COMPUTER GAME

THERE WAS A MONSTER inside the walls. Ursula, tucked up in her cardboard bed, thought she could hear it scratching, just inches away. She was not afraid of it because she made a point of not being afraid of anything, but it was getting harder now that she knew it was growing.

Ursula shared one gloomy room with her father, Mr Meager. He was the caretaker at Arthritis Hall. This morning she was pretending to be asleep while he prepared her special breakfast. She burrowed down under

7

her newspaper blankets, all warm and cosy. That was when she heard it: a word spoken right next to her ear. It was quiet but quite distinct.

"Juice." It had to be the monster, though the voice didn't sound very monstrous: it was small and metallic.

"Juice?" it said again, this time more like a question. The monster had never spoken before. Did it know she was there? Was it asking her?

"Wakey, wakey," wheezed Dad. "Happy birthday, petal, up you get."

He had laid a clean piece of newspaper on the table, lit a candle in a jam jar and arranged two chocolate biscuits and a grape on each plate, one for her and one for him.

"Come and get it, petal," he told her. "Got to be back at work in ten minutes or she'll have my guts for garters."

They ate in silence, the better to savour every delicious crumb. Then Mr Meager pretended to forget where he had hidden the presents and she pretended to believe him. Three packages this year, each wrapped in newspaper and tied up with an orange bow made from a rubbish sack.

"Start with the smallest," he advised. She eased the shell of newspaper off her first present. It was a packet of dandelion and burdock wine gums. They were the sort of sweets you or I might buy with our pocket money and chomp down in five seconds, but to Ursula, who had so little, they were a great treat.

8

The second package contained an adult's T-shirt printed on the front with the logo of a rock band and on the back with the tour dates from 1989.

"But it's your best, Dad," she protested.

"Go on," he urged. "I rinsed it through for you." She pulled it on over the vest, jumper, pyjama top, anorak and poncho she was already wearing. It fell almost to her ankles.

"Cheers, Dad," she said.

If you knew Mr Meager well you would know that the faint mauve bloom on his sunken cheeks was a blush.

The remaining present was a worry. It was altogether too smug, too jaunty. Ursula had known she would get the wine gums and the T-shirt but she didn't know what this was and it made her nervous. Her father didn't seem too sure about it either.

"Who is it from?" she asked suspiciously. He didn't answer, wouldn't meet her eye. "I bet I know who it's from," she grumbled.

"Go on, petal, just see what it is."

Ursula gingerly peeled back a section of the news-paper to reveal some very bright orange fur. For one mad moment she thought it was a Poo-Chi pet. There had been a huge craze for them at her school and there was nothing in the world she wanted so much as a real Poo-Chi pet. She ripped off the paper.

The thing that stood on their table, looking brand new and perky, well pleased with itself, was like a

9

Poo-Chi but it wasn't a Poo-Chi. It cocked its wea-selly head to one side and looked straight at her. Its eyes lit up.

"Hey there, Urse-w-la," it said. "Will you be my friend?"

"Who is Urse-w-la?" asked Ursula.

"Happy birthday to you," it sang. "Happy birthday to you, happy birthday, dear Urse-w-la."

She didn't wait to hear any more. She was gone.

On the morning this story begins, Duncan was in the back of his parents' car playing Poo-Chi Planet on his new phone. He was good at all computer games but Poo-Chi Planet was his particular favourite. He spent more time online playing Poo-Chi Planet than reading books, climbing trees and riding bicycles added together. He had just reached level twelve and Gizzmo, his online Poo-Chi pet, had a penthouse crammed to the ceiling with interesting and noisy things bought with the points he had won. There were chandeliers, farmyard animals, a wardrobe full of singing fish, scrolls of achievement, cups and prizes.

"Are you all right, Duncan?" asked Mum from the front seat.

He made a small noise. You might call it a grunt, but you couldn't possibly say it added up to a whole word. It was the smallest amount of sound you could make and still call it a reply. The truth was he was sulking. His parents were taking him to stay with his Great Aunt Harriet at Arthritis Hall while they went to Japan to build a tree house for a client. The smart new phone on which he was playing Poo-Chi Planet was his reward for not minding, although of course he did mind – and who can blame him? Anyone would sulk if they had to stay with a great aunt while their parents went to Japan, and this great aunt lived at Arthritis Hall, which made it ten times worse. I would rather go to the dentist than go there.

"Good old Aunt Harriet," yelled Dad from the front seat. "I used to love visiting her when I was your age. Always got some mad scheme on the go! You know what? I envy you, son, I really do."

Duncan didn't reply. There wasn't much to see out of the car window except a swamp where old sports socks, dead ducks and crisp packets lay in the mud. There was a sign which said, *NO*; just *No*. Any other words that were once there had long since worn away. There was also a camera on a pole watching the sign to make sure no one stole it. On the other side of the road a lorry thundered past. It was the first in a long line, all the same. Duncan read the slogan on the side: *GrumpO Industries, Working for You.*

Above the slogan each lorry had a huge picture of a happy family with shiny white teeth. They seemed to have just looked up from tickling each other and were going to get right back to it as soon as the photograph was taken. You would think, from the slogan and the picture, that the lorries contained something that would make people happy; but appearances can be deceptive. In this case the opposite was true.

It is only fair to warn you, before we go much further, that so much in this story is upside down, backwards, twisted, devious or just downright peculiar. It is not a story for the faint-hearted. It requires courage to face the unspeakably nasty things that are going to happen. It also requires maturity, foresight and an agile mind. If you are the sort of person who likes things to plod along in a predictable fashion from A to B then this story is not for you. I would suggest that you go and do something useful instead, like sorting out your socks.

"Turn that thing off now, Duncan," Dad called from the front seat. "We're nearly there." And sure enough Arthritis Hall rose above a line of greasy black pine trees. What a place it was! The sort of place birds came specially to poo on. It seemed to lurk, hunched up in the gloom, its gutters creaking, its gables sagging and clouds loitering around its upper stories, drizzling on everything below.

Duncan stayed in the back of the car pretending to take no notice while his dad tried to get the attention of someone inside the hall. He rang the bell, knocked on the door and beat his fists on the window. Nobody came.

"For goodness sake, we organised this months ago," Dad grumbled.

Nobody and nothing in that whole dismal pile seemed the least interested.

"We're supposed to be at the airport in twenty minutes," yelled Duncan's mother.

"I'm quite aware of that, thank you very much."

There was one moment, one heartbeat, when the whole dreary set of circumstances might have been avoided. They could have got back in the car, rearranged the trip and stopped on the way home, at a nice motorway service station, for pie and chips, but because of Mr Meager that moment passed. Instead of minding his own business as a sensible caretaker should, he listened to the raised voices by the front door. He peered down from the second floor window and wondered what he could do to help. It was soon established that yes, Harriet did live here and that no, she could not come down right this minute because she was doing something very delicate and complicated that could not possibly be interrupted;

and yes, Mr Meager would be happy to keep an eye on Duncan until the complicated thing was done.

I'm sure we all hope that Duncan's mother and father wrestled with their conscience and saw that they could not possibly leave their only precious child with a stranger in such a peculiar place. Surely they must see that it would not do. In fact, their car had reversed out of the drive before poor old Mr Meager had made it down to open the front door. Parents act all superior, like they never do anything wrong. They seem to think that just because they have things like car keys and pressure cookers and credit cards that whatever they do is automatically perfect.

"So you're Harriet's great-nephew?" wheezed Mr Meager. "Well, well, didn't know she had what you might call family. Doesn't seem the type." He tried to welcome Duncan with an encouraging smile but he wasn't very good at smiling. "And you're fixing to stay with her?" There was obviously something about this thought that Mr Meager could not process. "Like as a holiday or something?"

Duncan shrugged unhelpfully. He had decided to act as if the whole sorry arrangement was nothing to do with him.

"You sure that's a good plan, son, considering everything that's going on?"

No, Duncan didn't think it was a good plan. He hadn't thought it was much of a plan when Mum and Dad organised it months ago. However, since his parents had very definitely gone and he was here with his backpack, he thought they would just have to make the best of it.

Mr Meager hummed while he tried to work out what to do. If he didn't get back to work soon he would be in trouble. They stood next to each other in the entrance hall, silent and awkward, both unaware that they were being watched. It would be nice if I could tell you that the watcher was something or someone uncomplicated, like a monkey that had escaped from the zoo. A small problem that Duncan and Mr Meager could sort out together with a few phone calls and a bunch of bananas. In fact, the watching that was going on was very complicated indeed. There were at least two sets of eyes watching from two different places for at least two different reasons.

The elevator door slid open and there stood a tiny woman in a bright pink suit. The temperature seemed to drop with her arrival and small insects scrambled to get away, their knees knocking.

"Meager!" hissed the tiny pink lady, icily.

Mr Meager froze.

"Why aren't you working?" The question was asked in what sounded like a reasonable voice as if she really wanted information, but, before he could reply, she asked, "Is that a child?"

There was, of course, no denying that Duncan was a child.

"As you are well aware, we do not have children here."

The pink lady seemed to be quite sure that Mr Meager had caused Duncan to appear despite what the rules said on the subject of children and that he had done this to avoid work. Duncan tried to interrupt a couple of times to explain. He was a naive child who believed that grown-ups are basically reasonable people who will be reasonable if the facts of the situation are explained. The tiny pink lady ignored him, hissing at Mr Meager, chasing him back to work.

Ursula, who was also watching, was outraged for her poor father. She was stretched out on her stomach in the shallow space between the ceiling of the entrance hall and the floor of the room above, peering through a gap made by the ceiling light. It was not a very comfortable place to be, dark and full of little scuttling things, but Ursula didn't mind. She was used to it. Her hair was already decorated with dust and mouse poo. Her new birthday T-shirt was already dirty, snagged and rucked up around her middle.

Oh dear, poor Duncan! As soon as she had him to herself the tiny pink lady circled around him like a panther circling its supper, her pointy pink shoes click-clacking on the hard floor.

"My name is Mrs Linoleum Grunt and I am manager of this establishment," she told him. "Everything that goes on here is my personal concern—do you understand?"

He nodded cautiously.

Ursula leant in closer.

"Children are not at all welcome at Arthritis Hall, Great Aunt Harriets or no Great Aunt Harriets! We offer retirement apartments for gentlewomen. Do they want children cluttering up the place? No, of course they don't!" She pursed her lips at Duncan sourly as if it should have been obvious to him.

"You will be required to stay in one place at all times and make no noise what-so-ever."

There seemed to be nothing to say to this so he said nothing.

"You're very short, aren't you?" she added thoughtfully. Duncan was not very short, he was only quite short, which is another thing entirely; if he had been a different sort of boy he would have pointed out that she was only an inch or two taller herself.

"I shall need to know exactly what you have in your bag," she continued. "See-cur-i-tee." Duncan didn't move fast enough so she kicked his backpack with the toe of her pointy pink shoe. "Well come along, open it up."

There were two things of great importance to Duncan at the top of the pack: the charger for his new phone and Gizzmo, his original Poo-Chi pet.

"What is that?" she asked, pointing at Gizzmo as if he were a slug on a fairy cake. We all have failings, weaknesses or blind spots and Duncan certainly had a blind spot when it came to anything Poo-Chi. He firmly believed that if he just explained it enough everyone would find it as fascinating as he did.

Have you ever found yourself saying, "No, Grandma, when you buy your Poo-Chi pet from the shops they give you a code, and when you type the code into the Poo-Chi Planet website you get a version of your pet in the game. It's the same Poo-Chi pet, only flatter"? If the answer is yes then you have a lot in common with Duncan. It's a waste of time of course. Grandmas understand it perfectly well, they just like being tricky.

"He's a robotic pet," Duncan told Mrs Grunt. He flicked Gizzmo's *on* switch and carefully set him down on the floor.

"Poo Wee Chi," squealed Gizzmo, his eyes flashing as if delighted to be free again. "Wee Poo Chi." He charged at the skirting board on his little wheels, banging his head on it over and over again. Mrs Linoleum Grunt was horrified.

"It seems to be dam-age-ing my wall," she hissed.

Duncan went to collect Gizzmo but she stopped him.

"Phone," she demanded, her hand held out. Her fingernails, he noticed, were bright pink and filed to a sharp point. "That is a phone charger..." she pointed to his backpack, "so there must be a phone. Mobile phones are forbidden here at Arthritis Hall. See-cur-i-tee!"

Duncan could feel his phone, snug in the inside pocket of his jeans. He was suddenly quite sure he was not going to hand it over.

"You would have to be a cretin to carry a charger around with you but not a phone," she mused. "Are you a cretin?"

No phone meant no Poo-Chi Planet and how was he going to cope in this horrible place without Poo-Chi Planet? If she wanted it she would have to hold him upside down and shake him.

I will leave you to imagine how long Mrs Grunt held out her hand waiting for that phone, while Duncan, expressionless and blank, avoided giving it to her.

"I see," she finally hissed.

Ursula held her breath. Did he have any idea how much trouble he was in?

Mrs Grunt pulled a pair of pyjama bottoms out of his backpack; they were blue with red trains on them. She held them up at arm's length between thumb and forefinger as if they were somehow disgusting. She didn't speak, she didn't roll her eyes to heaven, she just gave a tiny sigh. Duncan blushed. They had been his favourite pyjamas but now he felt ashamed of them. She dropped them on the floor.

Next out was a sweatshirt with Chinese characters on the back.

"So what does it say?" she asked in a little sing-song voice which might make you think she was simply curious if you weren't paying attention. Of course Duncan had no idea what the characters meant. "Well come along, it's your top. You must know what it says. Does it, perhaps, say 'kill the old people'? I think they would find that upsetting, don't you? I think considering this is a home for elderly ladies they might find that in-a-ppro-priate." She dropped the sweatshirt next to the pyjamas.

Eventually everything Duncan had brought—his toothbrush, his T-shirts, his underwear—had been examined, found wanting and dropped on the floor around her feet. Duncan's cheeks were burning; he felt defeated, ashamed and furiously angry all at the same time. Gizzmo had stopped singing, his eyes had stopped flashing and he was staring sadly at the wall. Mrs Grunt picked him up and closed her pink claws over his face.

"And this," she told Duncan, as she click-clacked back to the elevator, "is confiscated."

Gizzmo had a penthouse crammed to the ceiling with interesting
and noisy things bought with the points he had won.

- 2 -

SEVERAL INTRODUCTIONS AND
ONE TERRIBLE ENCOUNTER

URSULA WATCHED DUNCAN'S humiliation with a
kind of grim satisfaction. She had been involved
in a private war with Mrs Grunt ever since she was old
enough to really dislike someone. Mostly Mrs Grunt won
their battles but every once in a while she managed to
land a blow. It occurred to her that if she could discover
what Mrs Grunt was going to do with the confiscated
Poo-Chi pet she could rescue it. Then she might decide
to give it back, or, considering whose birthday it was,
she might not.

It was very dark in the attic spaces of Arthritis Hall, dark but surprisingly noisy. The elevator that goes up through the building clanks away and the huge pipes gurgle and fart like the innards of a great dinosaur. You and I would hate it. We would feel horribly cramped and desperate to sneeze. We would worry about putting a hand out and touching layers of spiders' webs, or little dead things we couldn't see. But Ursula was right at home. Her dad had been caretaker at Arthritis Hall ever since she was a baby and while he worked she explored. She now knew more about the hidden dusty bits, the nooks, crannies and secret hiding places than he did. When she wanted to, and she often wanted to, she could move about Arthritis Hall like a ghost.

As she set off to crawl along the wooden beams to her favourite spyhole, the one just above Mrs Grunt's office, something moved, something just near her. A little scuttling thing. Ursula stopped still. It was probably just a mouse, she decided; there were whole cities of mice living in the darker bits of Arthritis Hall. She was not afraid of mice, she wasn't afraid of anything. The mouse, however, was terrified.

It screamed, *EEEKKKKK*. The noise was suddenly smothered. *EEKKKekkkkkkkeeeeee*.

She could still hear its frantic cries but much fainter, as if it had been trapped inside something. The blood seemed to drain from her limbs, she was shaking. What thing could it be, just an arm's length away, that could catch a mouse and muffle it in an instant?

"Juice," it said.

Up until that moment Ursula had half imagined that she had made up the thing in the wall, that it was just a nightmare that had leaked out of her head, but now she could feel it, right there.

She reached down to see if there was anything she could use to defend herself. Her fingers closed on something soft and hollow. She could feel feathers. A dead bird lying in a drift of dried leaves and old newspapers.

"Juice?" asked the thing in the dark.

"No, thank you," said Ursula politely, because she didn't know what else to say. She could still hear the mouse screaming but it was now a tiny sound, wrapped up and muffled. Something hit her on the side of the head, something that had been thrown. She made a noise like "Ohh" and her hand went up to her cheek though the truth was she was more shocked than hurt. Was the monster throwing things at her? Keeping one hand on the dead bird, she reached down with the other and felt about for the missile.

The thing that had hit her was about the size of a grapefruit, a little squashy and, oddly, a little warm. It did not seem to be disgusting or slimy or burning, so, feeling braver, she picked it up. Was it vibrating ever so slightly? Was it pushing against the palm of her hand?

Have you ever poked a frog or a porcupine that has been run over, and then, when its guts spill out, realised that it is just as dead and disgusting and slimy as you thought it probably would be? That is how Ursula felt when she understood what had happened to the mouse. The poor panic-stricken animal was somehow inside the grapefruit-sized thing: it was actually trapped inside. She dropped it, horrified.

"Juice?" said the monster, lurching forward.

She could feel it coming at her. With every ounce of her strength, she heaved the dead bird in the direction of that dreadful thing in the dark. She couldn't see but she could feel the bird's wings open as it arced through the air. There was an explosion of feathers and dust as it hit home. Everything was confusion and uproar. Ursula scuttled backwards as fast as she could, heading for a hatch a few feet behind.

When Mrs Grunt had gone there was nothing for Duncan to do but scoop up his things and stuff them into his backpack. He was just collecting his underwear from the floor when a very unexpected thing happened. A girl fell out of the ceiling in a cloud of dust and landed right on top of him.

"Are you all right?" Duncan asked as they picked themselves up. Although he thought that properly she should be asking him that question. She had done the falling and he had been the innocent party, the one fallen on. She didn't answer, she just scowled at him.

What a strange girl she was, dressed in all those layers of dirty clothes, caked in grit and dust, looking thunderous. Of course Duncan did not know that she had just had a nasty experience. It is hard to be polite when your head is full of monsters who wrap up small mammals and throw them at you.

She opened her mouth to say something but then closed it again. She seemed momentarily frozen, then she turned and fled.

"Hey," he called after her.

She stopped and turned back, scowling.

"What?"

There were so many questions he wanted to ask. In the end he chose a simple, practical one.

"Will you show me where my Great Aunt Harriet lives?"

Gizzmo was snoozing. He was still upright but his eyes were closed and a line of Zzzs rose up from his head like bubbles rising to the surface of a pond. Kobe was disappointed. He usually checked out the popsicle parlour at this time of day to see if Gizzmo or RatboyRyan wanted a chat; he sucked his popsicle thoughtfully. Obviously he didn't actually suck it, being a two-dimensional arrangement of pixels on a screen. He lifted it up to cover his mouth for a second, then, as he lowered it, the popsicle shrank in size and the little thermometers that stuck out like horns from his head, one labelled *energy* and the other *happiness*, both glowed bigger and brighter.

What to do? There was a possibility that boredom might occur.

All of a sudden, the bit of screen where Kobe had been dissolved into coloured squares before reforming into the same Kobe, the same Poo-Chi pet, but flipped upside down. His little horns of energy and happiness were now planted in the ground. Weirdly, his popsicle did not flip, it hung there, now pointing to his feet rather than his head. The Poo-Chi pets on the ice rink took no notice of Kobe's transformation but a Poo-Chi pet called Zhang, with a remarkable pair of yellow shoes, lowered her popsicle. In real life Zhang's operator would never have addressed a complete stranger but there are advantages to being only a two-dimensional arrangement of pixels.

Zhang says, "Perhaps it is a glitch?"

Kobe says, "Not glitch." The words now scrolled out from his feet rather than his head. He flipped back up the right way.

Kobe says, "Not glitch, is code. Muck with code make it happen."

Zhang lifted her popsicle up to her mouth for a moment.

Zhang says, "You changed the code?"

Kobe says, "Yes, is computer language."

Zhang says, "I am aware code is language for computer."

Now they had reached a point of agreement there seemed to be nothing else to say.

Kobe says, "What flavour you got there? I got mango and peppermint flavour popsicle. Got snake's eyes on it also."

Zhang says, "Dingbat pie flavour is my choice." She liked her food simple. Then, maybe for something to say, or maybe because she was genuinely interested, Zhang says, "Now you describe to me how to do the same."

Kobe says, "How to do what same?"

Zhang says, "Make adjustment to code."

You would think that Duncan and Ursula, two children alone in the greasy emptiness of Arthritis Hall, would find that they had a lot in common; that they would chat away happily, becoming firm friends. In fact Ursula found she couldn't speak to Duncan at all. She wanted to, rather badly. She wanted to let him know how much she admired him for standing up to the ghastly Mrs Grunt. She wanted to tell him about the monster in the walls but didn't want to at the same time. She opened her mouth then shut it again, the words just wouldn't arrange themselves into a useful pattern.

Duncan noticed a handwritten sign saying *Out of Order* pinned to the elevator door. Next to it the board that ought to have announced which apartments were on which floor simply said that reception was on the top floor and the executive helipad was on the roof; apparently there was nothing else at all on any floor in between.

"Why do you need an executive helipad in a retirement home for old ladies?" Duncan asked.

Ursula wanted to help, she really did, but there seemed no way she could even begin to explain.

They slogged up the stairs past broken windows, gobs of dust rolling around their feet.

"Where is everyone?" asked Duncan. "Where are the other old ladies?" They passed an empty flat, its door hanging open. Inside boxes were stacked against the wall. Boxes were stacked in the corridors. It was as if everyone had moved out, leaving their stuff packed and ready to be sent on.

"That's Harriet's," Ursula told him, pointing at an unremarkable number 11 door. "She's not as horrible as Grunter but she's not very nice." Then it occurred to Ursula that Duncan might be fond of his relative. "*I* don't like her anyway, though she's probably all right." Her first attempt at a conversation with him had ended in disaster.

"I don't think I've ever met her," said Duncan. "At least I might have when I was a baby. I don't remember."

Ursula tried to arrange her face so it would suggest sympathy and interest, but not criticism of Duncan or anyone related to him.

"Do you think I should knock on the door?" he asked.

She shook her head. "Don't even think she's there at the moment."

"What am I supposed to do then?"

There seemed to be no answer to this so he sat down on the floor, got out his phone and logged on to Poo-Chi Planet. At the ice rink Gizzmo opened his eyes. Lovely lovely Poo-Chi Planet, where crystal-coloured balloons bounced off the fish swimming in the lemon-yellow sky. Where pink snowflakes fluttered down on to the blue trees, speckling the sea horses hiding in their branches. Poo-Chi Planet where his online friends were waiting.

"What's that?" asked Ursula.

In reply he turned the screen so she could see Gizzmo bouncing around his tiny, lovely world. "Do you play?" he asked.

That was it exactly. Did she play? Of course she didn't play. She was Ursula Meager, wearer of other people's T-shirts, how could she possibly bring together what was needed in the way of money, computers, leads, plugs, understanding and the necessary bits of internet?

"Think it's stupid," she told him.

"Lots of people think that," admitted Duncan, thinking of his parents, "but it's really not. You can do puzzles, and your Poo-Chi pet gets prizes. They can buy things from the different shops and make things and you can talk to your friends if you want to." He talked about its advantages as if she was hesitating between Poo-Chi Planet and any one of the many other fun and educational computer games.

"Stupid," mumbled Ursula, though her gaze never left the screen.

A wave of sorrow broke over Duncan as he thought of real Gizzmo, his proper Poo-Chi pet.

"That pink woman took him, do you think she'll give him back?"

Ursula shook her head. Obviously Linoleum Grunt was never voluntarily going to do something nice. Had he not been paying attention?

"You've still got that one," she offered, pointing at on-screen Gizzmo.

Yes, he still had on-screen Gizzmo, that was better than nothing; but before Duncan could find a way of saying this, Ursula had gone.

It had occurred to her, as it may have occurred to you, that even though she didn't have a fancy phone, and didn't know her way round Poo-Chi Planet, there were things she could do that Duncan couldn't. She knew how to find her way in and out of anywhere in Arthritis Hall. While he was busy in the game, spending his tokens on a variety of moustaches in the candy-cane-coloured shop, the real door behind him swung open. And there, on the inside of Great Aunt Harriet's apartment, looking rather pleased with herself, was Ursula.

Ursula pushed the lid off a dustbin and climbed out.

-3-

A PROBLEM WITH A GREAT AUNT
AND A TIMELY RESCUE

T HERE WERE NO china dogs or dried flowers in Great
Aunt Harriet's apartment but there was just about
everything else. Along the walls were workbenches piled
high with junk of every kind. Among the wire and tools
and jam jars and cables, Duncan spotted a half-eaten
sandwich, a glass eye and a musical saw. He could also
see the insides of a washing machine, half a tuba, a
machine to forge bus tickets and dangerous chemicals
from under the sink.

"Wow!" said Duncan. Then "Wow" again.

There was a bacon slicer wired up to a metronome and a miniature motorbike in a bottle. There were blue worms crawling out of plastic containers and the skull of an okapi. There were doorbells and bicycle bells and ship's bells, and a bucket labelled "stem cells—do not spill". It was easily the most interesting mess Duncan had ever seen.

"She should tidy up," said Ursula.

"Oh no, I don't think she should."

Ursula was surprised. She had never actually been in Harriet's apartment before but if she had she would not have been impressed. Harriet was just another one of those vicious old ladies that plagued her life—she was best avoided.

Duncan stared at the walls of the apartment. Where there might have been flowery wallpaper there were diagrams, sums, instructions, suspicions, lists, notes, jottings, formulae and tables, a clock showing the time in Reykjavik, and a recipe for glue pie. He stared at a detailed drawing of a mechanical armadillo.

"That's brilliant," he said.

"Is it?" She sounded surprised.

"Did Harriet invent that?"

Ursula shrugged. "Dunno, maybe. I suppose she does invent a lot of stuff." Perhaps where Duncan came from it was unusual for old ladies to invent mechanical armadillos. "When I was little they wanted a way to get messages and parcels around the hall. She put in tunnels

36

between all the apartments. She made a sort of robot postman but more like a... a..." She trailed off. What was it like? She remembered as a toddler the fear and fascination those lumbering things caused her as they loomed out of the darkness. The triumph she felt as they went wrong, collapsing in a wheezing heap. "Nobody uses them any more," she added.

Duncan examined a diagram of train tracks converging on a single station, or maybe they were nerves coming together in the spinal column. Then there was a huge drawing of a primitive sea creature, or maybe it was a river system showing the small tributaries and little streams coming together in one great flow of water. He didn't know what he was looking at but he was impressed and intrigued. He was starting to think that his father might be right: staying with Harriet might be very interesting.

"Is she a genius?" he asked, picking up a scale model of the submerged city under Lake Baikal made from toffee.

"No," said Ursula, who had seen Harriet pick her nose on more than one occasion.

Then a number of things happened all at once.

First the door in the corner of the room, that neither of them had noticed, flew open and Harriet, red-faced and furious, glared at them. Then Duncan dropped the model so that it broke between the tiny toffee bus station and the tiny toffee concert hall.

37

Harriet was roaring things like "How dare you interrupt?" and "thieves" and "outrage", but at the volume of a jet engine so that it was hard to pick out individual words from the wall of noise. Ursula put her hands over her ears and shut her eyes. Duncan protected his ears but didn't shut his eyes so he was the one to notice something moving in the gloom as the door in the corner shut behind his great aunt.

Even if she had not been furiously angry, Harriet was no one's idea of what a great aunt should be. She was very tall and she had huge hands. Now, red-faced and steaming, the long grey hairs of her eyebrows fizzing with rage, it felt like she turned the room, which had seemed normal size, into a cupboard. And who wants to share a cupboard with a furious great aunt? No one, that's who.

Zhang's operator was a clever Chinese girl living in a high-rise block in Shanghai. Her kind of cleverness was about watching and paying attention, which is a lot more special and important than it sounds. Zhang was not her real name, of course, as they always warn you on Poo-Chi Planet, it is not safe to use your real name for your character in the game. She was only supposed to play on Poo-Chi Planet when she had done all her homework, swept the floor, tidied up after the evening meal and laid her clothes out for the next day—and then only to practise her English. That was the theory anyway.

"Just doing a bit more geometry, Grandma," Zhang sang out as she whizzed around the Poo-Chi Planet ice rink. Then, as she stormed through the puzzle palace, "Sorry, Grandma, just finishing this fascinating article about the history of the Tang dynasty."

Kobe from Kenya had a very different way of being clever. He was obsessed with finding out how his Poo-Chi pet worked. He had chosen Kobe for his Poo-Chi pet's name because of a footballer he liked when he first joined Poo-Chi Planet, though the footballer had long since moved to Europe and got slow. Kobe took over the old computer that his dad had running in his garage in Nairobi and he added other screens and extra memory; always Poo-Chi Planet on one screen, the code that created it on another. Even in the early afternoon, when it was almost too hot to breathe, Kobe wouldn't stop. He chopped the code and squeezed it and cut it in half. He put Ps where all the Fs should be just to see what happened. He put 5s where all the 8s should be because why not! He crashed it again and again, pulling it apart to see how it worked.

Zhang was sometimes terrified by the chaos of his method but she watched and listened and noticed the rules that seemed to be appearing.

Harriet had clearly forgotten that Duncan was coming though some memory of the arrangement did seem to float to the surface of her brain as he explained who he was. But understanding why he had appeared in her living room and accepting that he should stay there were two different things.

"We're too busy at the moment," she explained. "I can't possibly stop work now. You'll have to go away."

Ursula was disgusted by Harriet's bad manners. "You can stay with me and Dad if you want," she offered.

"That's it, yes," Harriet urged him. "Go and stay with them."

Ursula went to track down her father and let him know about the arrangement while Harriet, happier now that she was soon to be rid of her unwelcome guest, prepared to stop thinking about him.

"Don't touch anything in here," she said as she ground shards of toffee into dust with her steel-capped boot.

"You can do what you like in the rest of the building but don't touch anything in here. There's an activity room somewhere, they have a television." She offered this as if it were a brand-new piece of technology bound to delight a child. "Go there!"

"I thought I was supposed to wait here for Ursula."

Harriet glared at him. He was trying to trick her, she felt quite sure, she just couldn't work out how. His attitude showed exactly why it was better not to have dealings of any sort with young people. Without another word she turned and stomped off, banging the apartment door as she left.

Alone in the apartment, Duncan explored for a bit, then played Poo-Chi Planet for a bit longer. Minutes turned to hours and still Ursula didn't come. At one point he thought he heard a noise so he got up and looked up and down the corridor for Ursula but there was no one. Perhaps the noise had come from somewhere else. He looked again at the door in the corner. There was a sign on it that said _No Entry At All_ underlined with green ink. When Harriet had come roaring out of that door he had seen something move behind her, he was sure he had. He found an ear trumpet among the vast mess of rubbish on the benches in Harriet's front room and held it against the door. He could hear nothing, except maybe a faint buzz like a generator. He shrugged and, as evening lumbered towards Arthritis Hall, he plugged in his phone to charge and returned to Poo-Chi Planet, always a more interesting and nicer place than the real world.

It was dark when Great Aunt Harriet finally returned.

"What are you still doing here?" she demanded. "I suppose Meager sent you packing! I don't know why he thinks he can dump his problems on me!"

This was so monstrously unfair that Duncan felt he had to stand up for himself.

"You told my dad I could stay with you!" he insisted.

There were a lot of curses and appeals to the Almighty from Harriet—old ladies are terrible swearers—but eventually she found Duncan a camp bed to sleep on. It was stamped *Property of the Korean Army*. Space was cleared for it in the windowless box room between stacks of tinned mackerel and drifts of plans, maps, blueprints and a broken glass harmonica.

"In there," she ordered, banging the door shut after him so hard it rattled.

Later, as Duncan lay on his camp bed, he could hear Great Aunt Harriet next door watching a documentary about spiders: in particular, the way the spider shoots out a thread of silk in which to wrap its still-living prey. She kept rewinding and playing the same section over and over again. Was she trying to invent a mechanical spider? Duncan heard it so often that night he felt he must know it by heart.

In the end Ursula had not mentioned the plan to rescue Duncan to her father. She had asked herself what Duncan would think of the single gloomy room she shared with her dad. How would he feel about sharing her narrow newspaper bed? Would he be OK about changing his pants while she and Mr Meager turned around and closed their eyes? If there was anything Ursula hated more than being looked down on, it was feeling that her father was being looked down on. So, just in case, Duncan must not be allowed to see her home. Perhaps if she could rescue Gizzmo for him he wouldn't mind so much being stuck at Harriet's.

That was why, a little later, in the gloom behind Arthritis Hall, Ursula pushed the lid off a dustbin and climbed out. She was the colour of mud from top to toe and her hair was decorated with soggy Rice Krispies and pieces of bacon rind. As she clambered down, a black bin bag fell to the ground and split open. She gave a grunt of joy and scrambled in the rubbish, emerging triumphantly with a handful of brightly coloured fur, the remains of Gizzmo, Duncan's Poo-Chi pet.

Mrs Linoleum Grunt, who had been waiting for just the right moment, snapped on her torch. She let the beam travel over Ursula, examining every stain, every unhygienic inch.

"Dear, dear, dear," she said in her little sing-song voice. "I think I have caught myself a burr-gurr-lurr." Ursula held Gizzmo behind her back. "That is a con-fiss-cated item," continued Mrs Grunt, "and you have been found in possession of it. That is stealing!" She spoke slowly, clearly. "Now, give it to me." The girl did not move.

"I suppose I had better telephone the policeman to come and put the burr-gurr-lurr in prison." Mrs Grunt shook her head slowly, sadly. "Such a young burr-gurr-lurr. Such a bad daddy to let his little girl steal from bins. I'd better tell the nice policeman about the bad daddy. I expect he'll lose his job when his little girl goes to prison."

Ursula knew what she must do. She must hand Gizzmo over. She thought of Duncan and the way he had not handed over his phone.

"Come along!" snapped Mrs Grunt.

Ursula bent down. She reached thoughtfully into the broken rubbish sack, then she threw. A ball of week-old fish guts slammed into the side of Mrs Grunt's nose then descended down the front of her pink suit, leaving streaks of grease and a smell that would make a hippopotamus faint.

Ursula clutched Gizzmo close and ran. What a joy, what triumph. She felt like she would explode. If there is one day in the year when you can do what you want, not what you should, and worry about the consequences later, that day must be your birthday.

Online Gizzmo, untroubled by what was happening to his real-world self, was going round the puzzle palace collecting his daily tokens from the games. After many months of practice Duncan knew exactly when to stop, when to click, and when to swipe sideways; he worked with all the vacant efficiency of a teacher marking home-work while drinking beer.

At the Poo-Chi Planet ice rink he noticed RatboyRyan, a big blue Poo-Chi pet and a particular friend.

Gizzmo says, "What you doing, RatboyRyan? I've been dumped in this weird place for the holidays."

RatboyRyan says, "That's a bummer, you should bust out of there!"

RatboyRyan whizzed around in a corkscrew motion. It was night-time in Australia where he lived, and RatboyRyan had been in bed for some time. He had

Poo-Chi Planet playing on his phone while, on his laptop, he was chasing the soldiers of the dark empire down the corridors of a partially destroyed space hulk. RatboyRyan was really very good at computer games. His parents had already told him twice to turn off and go to sleep but he couldn't sleep, he felt as if he was fizzing.

Kobe says, "Violence is not a good answer."

RatboyRyan says, "Wasn't sayin' violence, mate. Bustin' out ain't violence. Is it, G?"

RatboyRyan often referred to Gizzmo as G, as if it was too much trouble to type the whole name.

Kobe says, "Correction, not violent."

In an attempt to lighten the mood Duncan typed...

Gizzmo says, "It's weird. S'posed to be old ladies here but no old ladies..."

"Here come the Googleys, the Googleys." Their conversation was interrupted by an advert, one Duncan had not seen before. "Get Yourself a Googley. A Googley is Great!"

Duncan swiped it away.

Kobe says, "Where have old ladies gone?"

Gizzmo says, "Don't know, just got here. Just a few old ladies but lots of boxes."

Kobe says, "What's in the boxes?"

RatboyRyan says, "Maybe old ladies in boxes chopped up."

Gizzmo says, "Will find out and let you know."

Kobe suddenly disintegrated into a tiny flickering cloud of pixels before reappearing, now four times the size, coloured pink and with the right side of his head scooped out. Neither Gizzmo nor RatboyRyan paid this any attention, they knew how Kobe loved to muck about with the code. However, a little Poo-Chi pet with remarkable yellow shoes was paying attention. A great long stream of code spewed out from what was now Kobe's belly button. This dark cloud of numbers and letters was highlighted, copied, cut and pasted into a space above Zhang's head. It all happened so fast it seemed to flick between them. A moment later Zhang gave a shiver and turned herself into a large, pink Poo-Chi pet with the left side of her head scooped out; then she turned blue, then orange. A few more exchanges and both Zhang and Kobe were circulating through the three colours like arcade lights.

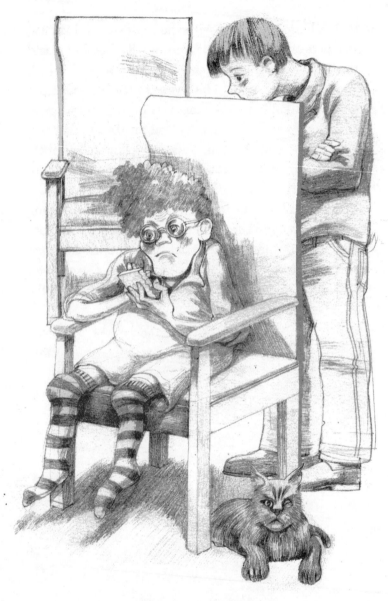

*Duncan found a tiny old lady playing a
computer game on a handset.*

- 4 -

WATCHING AND DISAPPEARING

A FTER A NIGHT spent dreaming of spiders, Duncan woke to an empty flat. Harriet was nowhere to be seen though the nature documentary was still playing behind the locked door. After sucking on a piece of toffee from the broken model for breakfast, Duncan filled his pockets with more emergency toffee and set out to explore. He wandered the empty corridors of Arthritis Hall looking, forlornly, for something to do. Staying out of Harriet's way while also avoiding the fearsome Mrs Grunt didn't offer many possibilities. He stared out of the grimy windows. He picked at a photograph of a fat sheep taped across a crack in a pane of glass. Maybe that girl would turn up again, that would be something. He pushed at the door of an apartment and it swung open but there was no cheerful grandma inside doing crossword puzzles and watching a programme about murder. Just another empty apartment full of boxes.

In the Operations Room, Mrs Linoleum Grunt ran the tip of her little pink tongue round her sharp little teeth as she watched a row of screens showing Duncan from different angles.

"That child must be watched," she hissed as she clipped the ear of the white-coated technician next to her. "I will not have that child sab-o-tarj-ing the project, are we clear?"

The elevator door opposite Duncan suddenly slid open and he found himself staring at a boy about his own age. This boy was very good-looking in a pale, elegant sort of way. He was wearing clothes that were actually very expensive but trying to look like they were nothing special, and he had lovely shiny hair that was better than other people's hair. The boy looked at Duncan. He seemed disappointed to find him there.

"Not this floor, Nathan," said a woman behind him who was loaded down with bags. Nathan shifted his gaze to a spot just above Duncan's head and stepped back into the elevator. Duncan just had time to notice the plush interior before the doors closed and the *Out of Order* sign reappeared.

50

On the next floor Duncan stumbled across the Activity Room. He was not impressed. It was certainly big but all it seemed to contain were a lot of high-backed chairs and a huge television showing a programme about soup. He thought he heard something snuffling but he couldn't see where it was coming from. Maybe it was the cat, dozing like a dusty old hoover bag in one of the chairs by the radiator. There was no one or nothing else.

At least that was what he assumed until he heard an electronic *bleep, blurp bleep*: a friendly, familiar noise. Following it he found a tiny old lady, wearing thick pebbly glasses and football socks pulled up over her knobbly knees, playing a computer game on a handset. She was slumped so far down into a high-backed chair that she was all but invisible from behind.

Duncan watched and waited but the old lady didn't look up from the screen, didn't seem to notice he was there. He moved a bit nearer. The plinky plonky music rattled on and Duncan realised that he knew the game. It was one of his favourites. He was itching to play.

"Can I have a go?" he asked the old lady.

"No," she said. She didn't even look up. Duncan moved to the chair next to her shoulder. Wow! She had a score of 1,700. Much more than he had ever managed.

"I've played that game," he told her. "My best score is 740."

"My best score is 13,860," she told him. "Which makes me nineteen times better than you."

Duncan smiled weakly. Perhaps, if he was quiet, he could just sit here for a bit and listen. The plinky plonky music felt comforting and there really was nothing else to do.

The television, which had been murmuring quietly to itself, suddenly started to shout.

"Here come the Googleys, the Googleys!" screamed a chorus of children, and on screen was a strange new toy. It looked like a fat, orange, cross-eyed weasel, not a patch on a Poo-Chi pet.

"My Googley, sooo cool!" yelled a boy, thrusting his toy out at Duncan.

"My Googley, soooo cute!" A girl dressed in pink held her Googley up to her face and hugged it against her cheek. She had a soppy, delicious expression.

It is sort of cute, I suppose, thought Duncan.

"My Googley, sooo much fun," declared a pale boy sitting in a wheelchair. He was looking into the face of his Googley and he was filled with joy. His lips trembled, his eyes were moist and his face was distorted with happiness. Through the television he turned a radiant smile on Duncan and Duncan stopped dead! He couldn't believe it. The boy looking out at him was the exact same boy he had just seen in the elevator. That boy had not been in a wheelchair, nor had he been particularly smiley, but it was the same boy, it was Nathan!

"I saw that boy," Duncan told the old lady. "That boy on the telly, he was just here!"

"Rubbish," said the old lady. "You must be mad."

I don't know if you have ever seen someone from the television in real life. It's not something that happens every day. If the old lady didn't believe him, he would find someone who did.

"I saw that boy," Duncan told the cat. It yawned; cats are not generally impressed by famous people. Duncan was just about to reach out and scratch the cat behind the ear. An innocent thing to do, you would imagine. He wasn't even really thinking about the cat, rather he was wondering what a boy from an advert for Googleys might be doing in Arthritis Hall. Why come to this grim, heartless place if you didn't have to? Let's just take time to notice the ordinariness of Duncan's gesture because once finger reaches fur, all hell is going to break loose.

In bustled Mrs Grunt.

"Is he bothering you, Mrs Pettigrew?" she called across to the little old lady in her sing-song voice. Mrs Pettigrew ignored her. "Don't you worry, I'll handle this." She bore down on Duncan like a guided missile and snatched up the startled cat, clutching it to her bosom. "Cat abuser!" she spat at Duncan. "How dare you!" She seemed choked with anger, making a great effort to control herself. "The old folks are very fond of Pork Pie," she hissed. "And I thought I told you to stay in Harriet's apartment. Criminal! There, there, darling," she soothed the cat. "You're safe now."

"I didn't do anything," Duncan pointed out, trying not to react to her absurd accusation, keeping his voice level and reasonable.

"Didn't do anything!" repeated Mrs Grunt as if this was an absurd idea. "Hah! Tell that to the police! They're coming right now! There's plenty of evidence against you, boy! It's all been logged." She turned on her heel and marched out, taking Pork Pie the cat with her.

Duncan could not help feeling that the whole world was a bit more mad than he could cope with. What was Mrs Grunt talking about? Evidence of what? Logged by who? Surely she wouldn't actually call the police but what if she did? A grown-up can invent any bonkers pile of nonsense and they will always be believed before a child.

There was a small explosion. It was actually quite a fuzzy, ordinary noise. The only thing that was not ordinary about it was the place it was coming from. It seemed to come out of the wall.

"'Scuse," said a familiar voice. "Sneezin'," it continued. "Allergic to cats."

"Is that you?" he asked the wall beside him.

"Might be," replied Ursula.

"Are you stuck?" he asked.

"I'm not stuck." She was indignant. "I'm hiding. I just don't want *her* to see me," she added, as if he might not know what hiding meant.

"Who? Mrs Grunt?"

54

"Old Grunter! I hate her, she's after me at the moment because I took something. She wants my guts for garters."

Duncan was pleased to think he wasn't the only victim of the fearsome Mrs Grunt but he still had a nagging feeling he was missing something, something important. After all, most children who want to keep out of the way of an angry adult retire to the back of the wardrobe with a comic. They don't crawl right inside a wall.

"Why do you have to hide in there?" he asked.

"'Cause of the cameras, obviously!"

What cameras? Were there cameras in Arthritis Hall? Were they watching him now? He looked wildly around the Activity Room, new suspicions forming.

"Are they watching everything?" His voice had dropped to a whisper.

"'Course, Grunter says it's see-cur-i-tee." Her tone implied that everybody knew this was a normal hazard of everyday life.

"Are they watching me now?"

"How did she know you were messing with Pork Pie? She's watching you. She's always watching."

A white-coated technician on the top floor sat in front of a whole bank of screens eating a fish paste sandwich. Some of the screens were showing cartoons but most showed what all those cameras, up and down and in and out of Arthritis Hall, were seeing. There was the front entrance, there was the back; and there was Mr Meager carrying a huge box down the stairs. The technician could also see Mrs Pettigrew in the Activity Room, still playing her computer game, and Duncan thinking. There was no sign of Ursula, she was being searched for but she was not being found.

If the technician had been bothered about such details, he would have noticed Duncan nodding to the bit of wall beside him, then glancing nervously around the room. It is true that discovering you are being watched is a creepy feeling, like finding your least favourite teacher under your bed wearing your pants.

On another screen Mr Meager tripped over something. It may have been Pork Pie the cat. He fell five steps and sat down hard as the contents of his box went flying. There are some people who find the spectacle of other people hurting themselves funny and the technician was one of these. He laughed so hard a piece of his sandwich went down the wrong way and he started to cough and splutter. In the end he had to fetch a drink of water. He was only gone a few minutes but when he returned Duncan had disappeared. The technician switched from camera to camera trying to find him but without success. The idea of having to explain to Mrs Linoleum Grunt that he had now lost both children burst over him like a cloud of wee.

On the opposite side of the street from Jerrard's, which you probably know is the grandest, biggest, most expensive store in the city, Mr Toffee Cheeseman was watching the customers come and go. He was looking for the distracted, the absent-minded, the high-spirited – the sort who would bung their wallet in their overcoat pocket, or drop their expensive phone on the top of their bag. It was windy so his shoulders were hunched up in his raincoat and his flat cap was pulled down low. Today Toffee Cheeseman was disguised as no one in particular.

If he picked you out as you walked down the street thinking about a sum, or what would happen if you poured gravy browning down your grandad's trousers, you might feel him brush past: an ordinary bloke in a flat cap. Probably you wouldn't notice him at all. However, when you came to spend those crisp notes you got for your birthday you would discover that they were gone. Things stuck to Toffee, which means Toffee was a thief.

This morning Jerrard's had a new display in their window and Toffee was finding it hard to concentrate on his work. He had never seen anything like it: little weaselly creatures with bright orange fur, goggley eyes and nasty little flat faces. Were they toys? They had been massed together in the window, a thousand of them, so that, from where Toffee stood, it looked as if one huge orange jellyfish had been poured into the window and squished up against the glass. If that wasn't disturbing enough, the jellyfish had a thousand pairs of eyes and each pair was watching.

Toffee could see a sort of ripple effect as orange heads turned to follow a passer-by as they crossed in front of the window. The passer-by, realising they were being watched, stopped, turned to look and walked back to check they were right. A group of boys banged on the glass to get the Googleys to turn in their direction. People took photographs on their phones and sent them to acquaintances in Alaska and Vladivostok.

There was quite a crowd gathering and Toffee was wondering if he might not be able to turn the situation to his advantage. He could mingle with the people and just see if anything stuck. But then a TV crew turned up and started bossing everyone about. That put the tin lid on it. There was no business to be done with a TV crew around.

"Don't look so glum, Toffee!" roared a slick-looking gent in a sharp suit, whacking him on the back so hard his false teeth nearly shot out.

"Blimey," protested Toffee. "You shouldn't creep up on a person." The Honourable Jago Lumsden ignored him.

"How's business, old boy?" he roared. "Didn't know you were still working this patch."

"Not much doing today," admitted Toffee. "Bloomin' cameras interfering with a man's right to earn a living."

Generally, if you say that a person is honourable you mean they do the right thing. They don't tell lies to get themselves out of trouble, or leave their clothes on the bathroom floor for their mother to pick up. But that was not why Jago was called Honourable. He never did the right thing if he could help it. The only reason he was called Honourable was that his great, great, great, great, great, great, great, great, great, great, great, great, great, great, great, great, great grandfather had done something unspeakable for a king who didn't want to have to do it himself. Which, I'm sure you agree, is not a good reason.

"Two words for you, old sport. Knitting and Circle!" With a flourish, like a magician producing a hamster out of a teapot, Jago unfolded the newspaper he had been carrying under his arm. Toffee recognised *The Burglar's Times*. He had read it since boyhood, mainly for the cartoons. But Jago was holding up the back page. Under a column called "Hints and Tips from the Lock-up" was "Dates for Your Diary". There Toffee read: "Any professional with a proven track record might wish to come along to the first meeting of the Arthritis Hall Knitting Circle for stimulating discussion and advice." At the bottom there was a contact phone number and a date.

"I have heard some very juicy rumours," purred Jago. "Very juicy indeed. Take my advice, old lad: get yourself some needles and wool, knit one, purl one. I smell new opportunities. And this," he tapped his bony aristocratic nose with two fingers, "never lets me down."

*The Googleys stopped singing and screamed
back. It was pandemonium.*

-5-

A VERY NARROW ESCAPE AND AN EXPLOSION OF GOOGLEYS

URSULA TOLD DUNCAN to meet her in the empty apartment she used as her second-best den. She thought she would not tell him about her best den until she knew him better, and maybe not even then. She described a door without a number that was invisible to both the cameras looking up the corridor and the cameras looking across the corridor. He would recognise it by the brass door knocker in the shape of a rabbit.

On the other side of that door Duncan found himself in a hallway blocked by a stack of boxes labelled with barcodes and strings of numbers. He tried pushing and shoving them out of the way and, after some effort, was able to make a space big enough to squeeze through.

He was in an apartment like Great Aunt Harriet's but more comfortable. The walls were decorated with photographs of buck-toothed grandchildren and huge, self-satisfied rabbits wearing rosettes. Duncan found a knitted rabbit sitting on a tower of toilet rolls next to the toilet, and yellowing pages of a recipe for butterfly cakes scattered over the flowery carpet.

He opened the door to the bedroom looking for Ursula. What he saw made his heart leap. There on the bed, eyes closed as if in sleep, was Gizzmo, his Poo-Chi pet. Dear old Gizzmo. Duncan couldn't believe it. He picked up his old friend to check him over. There was no doubt he smelt a bit funny, his fur was matted and dull; in fact he looked as if he had tried to take a shower. Duncan flicked his *on* switch and Gizzmo half opened his eyes.

"Chi," he said. He seemed very tired.

"Poo Wee Chi," replied Duncan sadly. But there wasn't time to worry about Gizzmo. He heard a nasty scraping sound right above his head. It began to rain down grit, dust and dead flies. This time he was able to jump clear before Ursula, in the shape of a small grey cloud, slithered down from the open hatch in the ceiling and landed, plop, on the bed. She shook off some old twigs, cobwebs and mouse droppings and glared at him.

"Hello again," said Duncan politely.

"Who said you could have that Poo-Chi pet?" she demanded, sounding rather more aggressive than she intended.

"Well, it is mine," he pointed out.

"Never said it wasn't but I'm the one that got it back off Grunter. That's why I'm on the run from her. Anyway, it's my den." Ursula had spent some time trying to wash Gizzmo to get rid of the smell of rubbish that clung to his fur, but washing just seemed to make him depressed. He could still be turned on, but he didn't do much once he was. She had decided to give him back and enjoyed thinking how pleased and grateful Duncan would be, how moved by her generous gesture. Now that was all spoilt.

"I was going to let you have it back anyway," she told him.

"Thank you," he said, rather formally.

Ursula had looked forward to being thanked but now that it was happening it felt rather embarrassing. She shrugged and gave Duncan a tour of the apartment, explaining why it qualified as her second-best den.

"Front door blocked from grown-ups, they're too big to get past that load of boxes in a hurry. Three other ways in and out. Bet you can't guess where they are."

"The hatch in the ceiling," he suggested but he didn't have anything else to offer. She led him into the kitchen and opened what looked like a cupboard door. Duncan found himself peering down a wide tube into bottomless blackness.

"It's a chute where you put bags of rubbish," she explained. "It goes down to the bins at the back." It dawned on him that she was suggesting a real, fragile person might willingly climb into that black hole. There was nothing in the world, Duncan believed, that would ever make him do such a thing.

"There's cardboard to land on at the bottom, it doesn't hurt much," she told him breezily.

Their next stop was the sitting room. It must once have been very comfortable, perfect for an old lady who liked to put her feet up and have a nice snooze. Now it was stacked floor to ceiling with boxes, and Duncan could see nothing that might count as an exit.

"Who lived here?" Duncan asked.

"She was called Daisy," Ursula replied. "One day she was here. Next day she was gone and these had turned up." They were the same sort of boxes Duncan had found in the hallway, and indeed everywhere else in Arthritis Hall. He pictured old ladies being toppled into them and taped over; their helpless cries fading, their puny fists becoming still.

"You know the Armadillo Post?" asked Ursula.

"Great Aunt Harriet's Armadillo Post?" he replied, as if it was hard to be sure which Armadillo-based postal service she meant.

"Daisy was going to be the postlady. She was going

66

to sort the post and send it off. She made herself a hat with A on it to wear when she was working." Ursula put her hands on her hips and looked at him expectantly, one eyebrow raised. She obviously thought that this information should suggest something to him; it didn't.

"Exit number four! All the tunnels Harriet and Dad put in for the post meet in here. Dad made a hole in the back wall by the fireplace. You can get anywhere from this room." Duncan didn't like to say anything but there was an obvious problem: all those boxes between them and the back wall. Ursula dropped to her knees and shoved one of the boxes in front sideways, revealing a box-shaped tunnel behind.

"Made it myself," she told him proudly. "It goes right back. Brilliant, isn't it!"

To make sure he appreciated just how tunnelly it was, she crawled in. Duncan hoped that he wouldn't be expected to follow. What if all those boxes collapsed? A person might be trapped underneath. He picked nervously at the tape on one of the boxes. It was printed, he noticed, with the logo of GrumpO Industries. He remembered his conversation with Kobe and RatboyRyan, and his promise to find out what was going on at Arthritis Hall, and it occurred to him that he might open one and take a look inside.

"So what happened to Daisy?" he called to Ursula. Quietly he prised up the end of the tape.

"Don't know." Ursula's voice was muffled. "One day she was here, then she was gone. She used to make me cakes, she was like a real grandma."

"So what do you bet is in these boxes?"

Ursula didn't answer.

He pulled and the piece of tape peeled off in one satisfying strip. "Could be old ladies' stuff, rabbits maybe... knitted rabbits. Maybe actual old ladies." He felt a thrill of horror as he imagined finding dead old ladies inside, perhaps bits of dead old ladies, maybe their grisly old dead faces smiling up at him. He imagined reporting what he had found to his friends on Poo-Chi Planet.

Gizzmo says, "Guess what I found today?..."

"Ursula!" he called. Could he hear something? Something scuttling. "Are you OK?"

The answer was not long in coming. Ursula screamed. It wasn't a little girly shriek. It was the sort of scream that makes all the hairs on your skin stand up, and every single bit of you pay complete attention.

Dropping to his hands and knees, Duncan could see her feet. She was kicking frantically, struggling against something. He caught her round the ankles and tried to pull her out but she wouldn't budge. She just screamed louder. Something had got hold of her and it wasn't going to let go. Her screams were suddenly muffled, as if her mouth had been covered, and her whole body was pulled away from him. What could possibly do that? Pull a whole person into a gap in the wall? His skin prickled with cold sweat. He felt sick.

Taking a deep breath he scrambled into the tunnel after Ursula. He tried to feel for what was holding her. It wasn't easy because it was pitch black and she was struggling frantically. Not teeth and claws as he had half expected. What he felt was metal and plastic. Something had trapped her arms and a three-pronged clamp, like a metal hand, held her by the neck. There was tape covering her nose and mouth. She was sucking, desperately trying to get air into her lungs. Duncan clawed at a great wad of tape stuck to her cheek. Whatever he did he couldn't get hold of it. She was going to suffocate right there beside him.

"Keep still," he hissed at her. She was able to stop herself long enough for Duncan to get hold of the tape over her mouth and pull. She gasped, her chest heaving, sucking in air. They lay there for a second, stunned and winded, trying to understand what was happening to them. That was when they heard it, a flat metallic voice right next to them. It was so close it might have been sharing a pillow with them.

"Juice," it said.

Ursula gave a little strangled yelp of fear and started to strain and pull against the clamped hand holding her down. Another clamp closed around Duncan's leg, squeezing it hard. He felt a wave of panic. Then, miraculously, the clamp around Ursula's neck released. It was as if the thing, whatever it was, had lost interest in her. Finally free, she scrambled back out of the tunnel. Duncan tried to follow but he was gripped too tight. *Try and distract it! Give it something else to think about; but what?* He felt around desperately and there in his pocket was Gizzmo. Duncan flicked the *on* switch and held Gizzmo out in the darkness.

"Poo Chi Wee," Gizzmo said. He flashed his eyes once. It was just enough light to show, for a fraction of a second, a strange yellow eye and a hard, curled form. A clamped hand closed around Gizzmo, crushing him. At the same time the grip around Duncan's leg slackened and he threw himself back towards the door.

There was Ursula, white-faced, holding the door frame with one hand and holding the other out to him. He grabbed it, then, stumbling, kicking, arms flailing, Duncan threw himself against the boxes, trying to collapse them. But if he thought that would stop the monster, he was wrong. The boxes began to heave. It was coming out after them. Duncan and Ursula threw themselves out of the sitting room and banged the door shut just as a three-pronged clamp drove through the wood, mashing it to splinters.

They raced for the rubbish chute in the kitchen. Ursula was first to climb in. She was shaking so much Duncan had to help her.

"OK?" he asked. She nodded and he let go. In a second she was gone. Duncan thought he could hear the wood of the sitting-room door splinter further.

"No choice," he told himself sternly. He climbed into the rubbish chute. It was a tight fit. All sorts of terrifying thoughts crowded in on him. What if he got stuck halfway, in the pitch black? Nobody would know he was there. What if the monster followed him? He closed his eyes, took a deep breath and let go.

In a town called Moose Jaw, which is in Canada, a young man called Ronald sold his very first Googley to a young lady called Ruby Mae Quinn. She was the most sophisticated and charming young woman that Moose Jaw had to offer.

"Is it for a niece or nephew?" Ronald asked.

Actually, Ruby Mae Quinn had rather thought she might keep it for herself.

"We will just have to wait and see, won't we," she replied mysteriously. Ronald laughed as if she had made a joke and the Googley joined in.

"Isn't it cute!" shrieked Ruby Mae.

"Hi there, purchaser," said the brand-new Googley. "We're best friends already." Ruby Mae laughed again. "Take me home, I want to be part of your family," the Googley insisted. "I love you."

It was then that Ronald had his idea. He got another

Googley out of stock and taught it to say: "Dear Ruby Mae Quinn, please go on a date with me." Then he taught it to repeat his name and phone number.

At the same time, another Googley trend was getting started. In an expensive hotel in the capital of a country that had better not be named, the first consignment of Googleys was rushed from the airport for the birthday party of a girl called Princess Venus Tuesday Spoon. She was the daughter of General Spoon, who owned one fifth of all the factories in that country and played polo with the president.

The Googleys were brought into the party on silver trays and arranged before the princess on her throne. The party planner had planned that it would be a lovely moment when the collected Googleys sang "Happy birthday, dear Princess Venus Tuesday", but it wasn't. As they erupted into song some of the younger guests, shocked and frightened by the sudden noise, burst into tears. The Googleys stopped singing and screamed back. It was pandemonium. Googleys, you see, just like young children, are programmed to learn by copying the humans around them; as far as they knew, screaming your head off was the thing to do at a birthday party.

The party planner, trying to rescue the situation, hurried on to where Princess Venus Tuesday Spoon was meant to hand each of her party guests a Googley as a thank you for helping her celebrate her special day, but she was indignant when it was explained to her what she was expected to do.

"No!" she bawled.

"Why not?" asked the party planner.

"I want them. They can't have them." She scowled bitterly at her guests. "It's *my* birthday."

Parents, officials and adults of all sorts were brought in to reason with her but she would not change her mind.

Ruby Mae Quinn had 1,743 friends on social media so, as soon as she discovered Ronald's Googley on her doorstep, she took a photograph and uploaded it. She added the tag: This cute little guy asked me for a date :) :) :) Wow!!

From such small seeds whole forests grow.

Soon Googleys were used to issue invitations of all sorts. They were also used to open supermarkets, threaten rivals, deliver sermons, cheat in exams, give the weather forecast, introduce the band and report the fat stock prices. There are rumours that they were even used to take secret instructions across borders to agents working undercover. Whenever you wanted something said, but did not want to have to be there yourself to say it, a Googley could do it for you. You can imagine the rude remarks a Googley might be taught to repeat from inside a school bag or a locker. There is a rumour that some boys in Columbia taught their Googley a rude song about a donkey and a bucket of rhubarb, then hid it behind the cistern in the teachers' toilets. One teacher became so angry when he couldn't find where the sound was coming from that he actually exploded, right there inside the cubicle.

Nathan licked his favourite low-calorie lime and chilli lollipop and thumbed through a magazine called Hair for Boys.

-6-

IN WHICH THE CHILDREN ARE DISCOVERED AND THE IMPORTANCE OF KNITTING IS EXPLAINED

U RSULA WAS WRONG. Shooting out of the end of a tunnel and landing smack on a pile of wet cardboard *did* hurt. Duncan rolled over and over before coming to rest flat on his back in a puddle. His brain, his heart, his lungs, his eyes, his tongue, his kidneys, all seemed to have been so shaken inside him that it felt like they would never find their right place again. But there was no time to get his breath back. Ursula was waiting for him, dancing from foot to foot.

"Come on," she urged, hauling him upright. "I live down here." She led him behind the bins and half pushed, half dragged him down a small flight of stone steps to a door choked with dead leaves and old plastic bags. It seemed to be a dead end but Ursula produced a key and, hand shaking, let them both in. It was the smell that hit him first. A wet earth smell mixed with old biscuit. Ursula turned on a light and he could see a single, dismal room, old bin bags of rubbish against the walls, a candle in a jam jar on the table and a few bits of furniture, perhaps stored here until they could be thrown away.

"Aren't we going to your house?" he asked.

"This is my house," she told him, flushing pink with embarrassment.

Duncan didn't know what to say. He was shocked. To him "my house" meant cosiness: armchairs, biscuit tins in the kitchen. How could anyone possibly live here?

"Sorry," he said.

Ursula would definitely have punched anyone else that had insulted her home; it was like insulting her father, it was like insulting her, but she could not punch Duncan; not now. Not after what they had just been through together. Without further comment she dropped to her knees and crawled under the table, disappearing behind the layers of newspaper covering it. Duncan wasn't sure what he was supposed to do until she snapped, "Aren't you coming?"

Being under the table was like being inside a tent. The buttery yellow glow of the torch showed a couple of cushions, a handful of books, some ornaments and a game of snakes and ladders.

"Borrowed these," she told him, moving a yellow china rabbit that must once have belonged to Daisy. "Dad says we shouldn't take things from the empty apartments but I think, oh well, nobody's using them."

"Why don't you go and live in one?" Duncan couldn't help asking.

"Grunter says they're needed for storage. She tells Dad he's lucky to have this."

They sat side by side waiting for the shaking to stop. They were both trying not to think about the terrible thing in Daisy's sitting room, but neither of them were succeeding.

In the end Duncan said, "It wasn't an animal, was it?"

She shook her head. Then she added, "It's getting bigger though." It was a relief to say it out loud.

"What do you mean, it's getting bigger?"

She shrugged. "It just is."

"You've seen it before?"

"Not seen it but..." She trailed off. "I think it's living in the tunnels, I think it's growing in there."

Duncan thought about poor Gizzmo held up as a sacrifice. He must have been mashed and consumed by now. Then he thought about his smartphone. It had been in his pocket all the time. He pulled it out, praying it had survived. There was Poo-Chi Planet, just as it should be. Thank goodness!

"Is it all right?" asked Ursula.

Duncan wanted to make up for what he had said about her home so, as a peace offering, he put his new phone into her hands. He even pretended not to mind as her grubby fingers closed around it protectively. He gave her a tour of Gizzmo's online world. There was his magnificent apartment. He let her move things around and even change the wallpaper; he could always put it back the right way later. He showed her the puzzle palace and the ice rink, the lemon-coloured sky and the shoals of flying fish. He showed her his friends chatting by the popsicle parlour. Ursula stared at it all, transfixed, delighted, willing it to make sense. Poo-Chi Planet was suddenly interrupted.

"Here come the Googleys, the Googleys," screamed an advert.

"They're the very latest thing," Duncan explained.

"Oh, they're boring," said Ursula. "I've got one of them." She crawled out from under the table and returned with a bundle of old newspaper. She peeled back the layers to reveal a real Googley, bright orange and perky. Duncan was amazed, and also a little confused. It seemed as if she had none of the things he considered essential for normal life, but she did have the very latest toy.

The Googley cocked its head to one side. "Will you be my friend?" it asked.

"Don't say yes!" Ursula warned.

"Why not?" asked Duncan.

"Don't say yes," commented the Googley in an uncanny imitation of Ursula. Duncan was astonished.

"It copies you," she told him; as if that wasn't clever at all, as if all toys more or less could do that.

Ursula played on Poo-Chi Planet, getting some good scores for a beginner. Duncan meanwhile examined this Googley thing. He moved his hand and the Googley moved its head, watching the movement.

"That's amazing," said Duncan.

"That's amazing," agreed the Googley, nodding its head to show agreement.

A thing made of metal and plastic that could move and sense the world around it. There was something else nagging at Duncan. Something he needed to remember. He made himself think back to Daisy's sitting room; to the moment he had looked back into the room and seen the three-pronged hand whip out from under the boxes on the end of a long cable. There was something scattered across the flowery carpet: the contents of the opened box.

"Those boxes, they're full of Googleys, aren't they?"

Ursula wasn't really listening.

"Product of GrumpO Industries, Googleys!"

"Probably," Ursula agreed. "Grunter would never have given me one for my birthday if she'd had to pay for it."

In a city tower block not far from Jerrard's department store the Googley TV marketing team had organised a meeting, but there was one person present who did not seem to be paying proper attention. He was to be the new channel's presenter. Nathan had his feet up on the chair. He was licking his favourite low-calorie lime and chilli lollipop and thumbing through a magazine called *Hair for Boys*.

"OK, kids," said a shiny-faced man to all the grown-ups in their dark suits. "We've got a lot of data to power through." He showed them a slide of a cheese divided into different coloured triangles and explained that some of the people who have heard of Googleys said they would watch Googley TV. Some of the people who have not heard of Googleys also said they might watch Googley TV. The phrase "Googleys rock" was the second most popular phrase used on social media sites about Googleys. He told them about a backlash by Poo-Chi fans, both on the internet and as direct action. Apparently in Warsaw and Rome Poo-Chi related graffiti had been sprayed across the windows of toy stores displaying Googleys.

The next bit was about Nathan; or rather the Googley-loving boy in a wheelchair that Nathan was supposed to be. He had a cheese diagram all his own, not that he bothered to look at it. Two thirds of those who were positive about Nathan's appearance liked his hair. Eighty-six per cent of those who said they intended to watch the launch of Googley TV said their enjoyment would be enhanced if Nathan dressed up as a Googley. Nathan had received 213 proposals of marriage and fourteen people had asked to adopt him.

"What do you think about that, Nathan?" asked the lady from the talent agency, who was rather embarrassed by his lack of interest.

Nathan looked over the top of the magazine and fixed her with a beady stare. He said nothing for a long time, which made everyone uncomfortable; it was a trick of his. Finally, he told her, "You can't make me marry any of those dorks." Everyone laughed as if he'd made a terrific joke but Nathan sucked his lollipop bitterly. "And there's no way I'm dressing up as a Googley for the launch, those things creep me out." He returned to his magazine as if the last word on the subject had been spoken.

A key turned in the door. Duncan nudged Ursula. The torch and Poo-Chi Planet were both snapped off. She looked at him meaningfully: *Don't move or make a sound.*

The footsteps coming down into the room were heavy and slow. Ursula relaxed.

"It's Dad," she mouthed to Duncan but she held a finger up to her lips to warn him to keep quiet. They listened while Mr Meager pottered about making himself a cup of tea.

"You under there, petal?" he asked.

"Don't say Urs-w-la," advised the Googley. Both children leapt on it and smothered it with the layers of newspaper.

"Playing with that thing now, are you?" Mr Meager tried to chuckle but it came out as a cough. "Thought you didn't like it," he said when he could speak again. He sat down heavily at the table, his knees nearly knocking against Duncan's forehead.

"'Spose you're staying in one of those dens of yours," he wheezed. "Good idea, you steer clear. I don't know what you did but she's spitting fire." He put a couple of biscuits on the seat of the chair next to him. Ursula reached up and grabbed them. She was about to cram them into her mouth when she remembered Duncan and passed him one.

"That lad's done a disappearing act," Mr Meager told his daughter. "She wants his guts for garters. You better stay out of his way, petal, you're in enough trouble without getting mixed up with him." Duncan and Ursula, squashed together under the table, exchanged looks. "Don't know what's up with her at the moment," continued Mr Meager gloomily. "She's worse than normal." Ursula patted her father's leg soothingly. "All I know is they've got something big happening tomorrow." He wheezed and slurped his tea. "If you do see that boy you let me know, petal. Maybe if we turn him in she'll leave us alone for a bit."

How did Duncan feel, an inch away from the knees of a man who would be happy to hand him over to the dreadful Mrs Grunt? The truth was that after the horrors of Daisy's apartment he felt very tired and desperate just to be ordinary; and anyway it was difficult to be scared of slow, wheezy, kind-hearted Mr Meager. Duncan curled up next to Ursula, his head on one of Daisy's rabbit-patterned cushions. He tried not to think, although he found it difficult. Best to concentrate on his mother's chicken pie. If he could have anything right now that would be his choice. He would have chicken pie and mashed potato on his lap in front of the telly. He would watch something silly with his mum and dad, they would laugh at it together.

The Googley, in its sleeping bag of newspaper, had also gone quiet, but it never stopped watching Duncan. Its beady eyes were always on him.

There is a wool shop on the Horseferry Road, one of a handful left in the city. These days most of the people who want to buy wool go to the big department stores in the city centre or they order on the internet. This wool shop is a sleepy, untidy place. There are knitting patterns for vests and tank tops hang from a washing line across the shop window. There is also a picture of a fat baby wearing a knitted bonnet secured under its chubby chin with a pearl button. It wears a matching knitted jacket with pearl buttons, knitted leggings and knitted gloves and booties. The poor thing is trussed up like a turkey at Christmas, entirely cut off from the world by wool. It's trying to smile but it's not fooling anyone.

It is this shop that was surprised by a number of unusual customers. A vicious-looking gent in a sharp suit arrived one day, just as the shop was about to close.

"Got any wool?" he demanded in hushed, urgent tones, checking over his shoulder for potential threats. Obviously they had wool.

"What kind would you like, sir?"

"Don't matter, any wool." It was hard to know what to do with this. "Come on," he urged, clicking his fingers at the shop assistant, "don't muck me about, just give me what other people have." He left with eight balls of mustard-coloured three ply and a pair of knitting needles that cost about five times what a more polite customer would have paid.

The next day there were a couple more, four or five the day after that. None of them seemed very interested in their purchases. Colour didn't matter, the weight of the wool was no concern of theirs. The owner and his assistant began to see that they could unload old stock they had long since despaired of selling. Several evil-looking thugs left with worm-coloured chunky or lime-green mohair.

"What we got to get this for?" one huge hooligan with tattoos across his knuckles demanded of his companion. "I 'ent going to knit nothin'."

"You don't actually have to knit anything," his friend explained, probably not for the first time. "It's a ruse, a plot, a plan. You don't have to knit, you just have to look as if you might."

There was one gentleman in a flat cap, however, who endeared himself to the assistant by asking lots of questions. He hesitated over a range of colours, wondering what would go with his eyes. He even asked for advice about the size of the needles he would need. Toffee Cheeseman might have paid for his purchases with a note he had liberated from a city gent's jacket pocket but he left the shop with a spring in his step. The world suddenly seemed full of new possibilities.

There was an impatient rap on the door.

"Shhh," Mr Meager hissed at his daughter.

"Shhhh," she mouthed at Duncan. Very few people ever came to visit Mr Meager and his daughter in their basement home, and the few that did always brought bad news. Duncan, Ursula and Mr Meager all ran through the terrible things that might be about to happen. Mr Meager was trying to work out which one of Mrs Grunt's instructions he had forgotten to carry out. Ursula and Duncan huddled closer. They were both imagining that the monster was out there, knocking on the door. They heard the scrape of Mr Meager's chair, his heavy foot-steps. They held their breath.

What happened next was both noisy and fast.

"Out of my way, Meager!" roared Great Aunt Harriet, her voice booming off the walls.

She reached under the table, grabbed Duncan and yanked him to his feet. She propelled him in front of her, holding him by the hair.

"Owww!" squealed Duncan.

"Blimey!" started Mr Meager, who was, of course, very surprised to see Duncan.

"No, you hang on!" roared Harriet, as if Mr Meager had protested. "Item one: this boy is a known cat abuser." She shook Duncan at Mr Meager menacingly. "He has been abusing Pork Pie, he has been creeping about taking things from empty apartments. A proven troublemaker! Item two is also under your table right this minute."

Item two, which probably meant Ursula, was just then crawling out. She and Duncan stared at each other, horrified. How could they possibly have been discovered? Great Aunt Harriet's voice seemed to get even louder, like a jet engine gathering itself for take-off. "Deal with it, Meager. If you don't, you know who will."

Duncan was yanked, pulled and dragged up the stairs and back along the corridors of Arthritis Hall. Great Aunt Harriet held a handful of his hair in her huge fist. It didn't help that she had extra-long strides so he had to practically run to keep up with her. It hurt worse than you can imagine. All Duncan could think about was preventing her from pulling his hair out entirely.

"Linoleum will sort you out in the morning," Harriet told him, as they reached her apartment. "Oh yes! Linoleum will have your guts for garters." She was obviously delighted by the idea.

It was only when he had been unceremoniously thrown back into the box room where he had slept the previous night, the door locked on him and several bits of heavy furniture dragged across the threshold to make a barricade, that Duncan remembered Ursula still had his phone.

*There was Ruby Mae and her Googley
giggling together on the sofa.*

-7-

TOO MANY GOOGLEYS AND THE RIGHT NUMBER OF POO-CHI PETS

I T TURNED OUT Princess Venus Tuesday Spoon wanted all those Googleys for a reason. She had a plan. Jacinta, her maid, had refused to iron her silver dress when she wanted to change into it ten minutes after she was due to leave for her birthday party. Jacinta had said, ridiculously, that there wasn't enough time to iron it properly considering they were already late. Princess must punish her. That evening she took all her Googleys into her private suite and taught them to say, "Jacinta is fat" and "Jacinta is smelly". Of course Jacinta was not then, and is not now, fat or smelly, but these are just standard insults; whether they are true or not is hardly the point. Princess had a very determined sense of right and wrong, especially when she had been checked or thwarted in any way, but she did not have much imagination.

When, next morning, Jacinta brought Princess's breakfast of scrambled egg and soldiers she was greeted by a deafening chorus of abuse from the orange weaselly ones. She shrieked and the breakfast went flying. Most of the scrambled egg caught the waking Princess full in the face. Some of it even went up her nose. It goes without saying that Jacinta was dismissed immediately but she didn't mind too much. Her sister got her a job crisping whelks, which was more fun and better paid.

After this Princess decided the Googleys were boring and they were left where they fell, like leaves that had blown in from outside. There were drifts of them in the office, in both drawing rooms, in the ballroom and the morning room; in the home cinema, the long gallery, the gym and all the bathrooms, even in the walk-in cupboard where the family kept their emergency supplies of lavender-flavoured coconut creams.

Three days after her birthday the Spoon family took their private jet to their private beach hideaway in Jamaica and all the remaining servants put on the family's nicest clothes and went out to celebrate their employer's departure. While they were out a gang of burglars got into the Spoons' penthouse apartment from the roof and took everything. They took all the porcelain, all the paintings, all the money and jewellery, all the rugs and furniture and clothes and computers; all the ski equipment, the polo equipment, the archery equipment, the diving equipment; the golden toilet roll holders and the life-sized bronze elk which had stood in the billiard room. This elk had its head raised and its teeth bared and it was looking at the goings on in the billiard room with an expression of appalled contempt. General Spoon had bought it when he thought he might be interested in art but, seeing it up close, he realised he wasn't. The burglars took absolutely everything apart from the Googleys and the lavender-flavoured coconut creams. Perhaps burglars don't like coconut creams.

When you learn about a thing, followed by another thing, it is only natural to assume that the first thing caused the second thing, but, of course, this does not have to be true. For example, a person might think that what happened to Jacinta caused the burglary in some way. General Spoon and the police certainly thought so, but was that right? If you heard that Father Christmas had covered all the world in a thick layer of yellow custard, and then you heard that all the elephants in India were trying to climb trees, you might assume that they were trying to climb the trees to get away from the custard, but that is not necessarily true. Maybe elephants like custard; and maybe they'd planned an

happen tomorrow and there was nothing you could do to stop it? Maybe you have to go to the dentist or you have detention at school; or maybe you are going to have to stand up in front of all your friends wearing a bonnet and a long dress with ribbons and explain algebra. You can feel the horror creeping towards you hour by hour, minute by minute. It becomes impossible to imagine that you can ever reach the future on the other side of the terrible, unendurable thing. If you have ever felt like that you will have every sympathy for Duncan.

One way of not thinking about what was coming was to think about what had just happened, but that wasn't much better. He pictured himself lying next to Ursula, his head on one of Daisy's cushions, smiling at her Googley, who seemed, somehow, to be smiling back. But thinking about being under Ursula's table led him to think about being discovered, and that led him to wonder how. There were obviously no cameras in that basement room. Had someone told Mrs Grunt where to find him? Was it Mr Meager? Was it Ursula? But how could Mr Meager have found out he was there? And anyway, how could he communicate the fact to Harriet? Maybe he and Ursula had been working together all the time. Was it possible that they had set up everything that happened in Daisy's apartment as a way to trap him? Duncan rubbed his bruised leg where the monster had gripped him with its metal prong. No! Ursula had not been acting, she had been truly terrified, and if anything in this insane place was real it was that monster.

Somewhere else in the apartment Great Aunt Harriet seemed to be watching a programme about the Peruvian mole. To be precise, she was watching the same part over and over again.

"This amazing animal, one of the shyest on the planet, can live its whole life without ever seeing daylight," breathed the voice-over. "Those scoop-like front paws mean he's perfectly adapted to life underground. In fact in a single year he can dig enough tunnel to stretch from Paris to Moscow."

There was a hush in which Duncan imagined the mole must be demonstrating his digging; his little nose twitching, snuffle, snuffle, his paws a blur.

"In this complex network of tunnels, different parts are used for different purposes. Here the mole has established a nursery, and here a laundry, and here these astonishing creatures have made a larder where they store their food of choice, earthworms!"

Snuffle, snuffle, snuffle.

"A Peruvian mole's saliva contains a special toxin. One bite and the earthworm is rendered senseless. It can be stored, paralysed but still living, for later consumption."

Duncan tried to imagine what it must be like to wait, paralysed, to be consumed. Perhaps, he thought, like waiting to be taken to see Mrs Grunt in the morning.

"Before eating the earthworm," the commentary continued, "the mole will squeeze it between its paws to force the collected earth and dirt out of its gut."

There were horrible squelching noises, licking and snuffling. It was disgusting. Duncan even thought he could hear a tiny scream as the earthworm was squeezed. He heard it so many times during the night that he knew, whatever happened to him in later life – whether he grew up to be an astronaut, or a television expert, or a drummer in a band – he would never not know about the eating habits of the Peruvian mole.

OboCurlyTops was a Poo-Chi pet with a problem. She was owned jointly and equally by twins living in Texas in the United States. One Poo-Chi pet with two operators is an arrangement that might have worked if they could ever agree on anything, but they couldn't. The name OboCurlyTops, which is not a good name, was an attempt at compromise. So was her outfit of black biker gear decorated with butterflies, a giant black moustache and sun bonnet. The others were used to OboCurlyTops falling silent in the middle of a conversation while the twins fought each other for control, but today they seem to have suspended their war.

OboCurlyTops says, "We're going to make Mom get us a Googley, they're neat."

Zhang says, "In what way are they neat? Are they tidy and well organised?"

OboCurlyTops says, "You r goofy."

RatboyRyan steamed across the ice rink to make his position clear.

RatboyRyan says, "Poo-Chis are the greatest! Googleys stink, they are rubbish. Don't bring one of them near me."

Gizzmo's eyes opened. He was awake but he didn't join in the discussion. He just stood there. Kobe turned to him.

Kobe says, "You found what happened to old ladies?"

Gizzmo didn't reply.

RatboyRyan says, "I'm going to get some paint and do all the windows downtown: Death to all Googleys. I don't care if they put me in prison."

Zhang says, "I have seen an advertisement for Googley. It appears to have very sophisticated manufacture. Must cost lot of money."

RatboyRyan says, "It's rubbish. Adverts are rubbish, they are rubbish."

Kobe says, "Is true they can do same again then do different? How is this?"

Gizzmo says, "B."

The other Poo-Chis waited politely to see if he would say more but he didn't. They had turned their attention to other important matters when he suddenly said:

Gizzmo says, "I TYPE HERE IT COME OUT There."

Ursula had found the button on the keypad of Duncan's phone that would allow her to turn off the capitals. All the other Poo-Chis were a little embarrassed. It was as if Gizzmo had never been on Poo-Chi Planet before.

OboCurlyTops says, "You like Googley toy?"

It took Ursula a minute to understand this was a conversation. She struggled to type fast enough:

Gizzmo says, "Millions here, but junk they are, BAD RUBBISH!"

The others were rather startled. Gizzmo seemed to have lost his usual steady, reassuring tone.

OboCurlyTops says, "How come u got millions of Googleys?" It seemed unlikely given they were the very latest thing and not easy to track down.

Gizzmo says, "In boxes here, every place, millions."

Kobe says, "Old ladies turned into Googleys, then put in boxes?"

Gizzmo says, "Might do same to Duncan."

Kobe says, "Not to say real name like Duncan or such same."

Gizzmo says, "GOt to HELP. HElp Duncan, HELP!"

Just outside the candy-cane-coloured shop that sells moustaches, I'm sure you know the place, between the puzzle palace and the ice rink, four Poo-Chi pets gathered around Gizzmo. Kobe, RatboyRyan, OboCurlyTops and Zhang all felt they wanted to do everything they could to help Duncan even if they should not know his real name.

Casey J's dressing room looked and smelt like a florist shop. After her concert in Budapest she had been given twenty-seven bouquets of flowers, thirteen cakes, several thousand cards, a jacket with a picture of herself made out of bits of chewing gum stuck on the back, a Googley and, most bizarrely, a very small horse who was obviously confused. It kept trying to back out of the room.

"What-do-ya-wana-do-with-it-all?" asked Casey's assistant. The tour employed a girl just to deal with all these gifts from fans.

"Flowers to the hospitals, cakes to the orphanage," intoned Casey, it was what they always did whether they were in Paris, Moscow, Tokyo or Dubai. In fact, cards of love from Casey to hospitals and orphanages all around the world had been written and stored away for just this purpose before the tour had even started nine months ago.

"The horse is kinda cute," said Casey. She sighed. "Better not keep him, I guess. Can you find a petting zoo or something?"

The horse was now rotating backwards with its eyes shut. It was trying, against all the odds, to retain its dignity.

"I'll keep the Googley and the jacket but dump everything else," she decided.

Three days later the drivers of the convoy of huge trucks containing all the equipment for the tour got a new message on their phones. Instead of heading down to the city where the next gig was supposed to take place they were redirected on to a ship at the nearest port. It might be said that those trucks, and all the very expensive equipment they contained, were never seen again, but that would not be quite true. If you know where to look on internet auction sites you can find them being offered for sale.

Sitting on the delicate white chairs was the meanest looking crew of villains that Duncan, or indeed anyone else, had ever seen.

-8-

SEVERAL WAYS TO GET RID
OF DUNCAN AND A CHANCE
MEETING IN A CUPBOARD

THE SHORT RIDE up in the elevator the next morning from Harriet's apartment to the very top floor of Arthritis Hall brought Duncan to an entirely new world. His very irritable great aunt had hauled him out of his camp bed only a few minutes after he had finally fallen asleep, or at least that's how it felt. She had complained loudly about the mess in the box room as if he was responsible for the swamp of nautical maps, blueprints and cross sections of nuclear bunkers, tins of mackerel and the bits of a broken glass harmonica that shared the space with him. She gave him a kick with her steel-capped boot and hauled him into the elevator.

Harriet's apartment was noisy and scratchy and chaotic. By contrast, everything here on the top floor was hushed and polished and shiny. Water trickled into marble fountains while the carpet swished politely and the air conditioning purred.

"Morning, Miss Harriet," said a pale young lady receptionist in a pale suit. She looked Duncan up and down doubtfully. "Is he for the knitting circle?" She consulted her clipboard.

"He's for Linoleum," said Harriet, finally releasing her grip on Duncan. "Sneaky little blighter! Best watch him. We don't want any unforeseen circumstances today!"

"No, we certainly don't!" agreed the pale young lady, taking a firm grip on Duncan's ear. "Best of luck with it all," she cooed. "We've all got our fingers crossed." Great Aunt Harriet lumped off to a door marked, *Laboratory— strictly authorised persons only*.

"Follow me, don't dawdle and don't touch anything," instructed the pale young lady receptionist.

She led him into a waiting room of pink and white splendour. Silver trees in silver tubs stood in between white buttoned chairs with delicately carved silver legs. Sitting on the delicate white chairs, looking less than comfortable, was the meanest looking crew of villains, crooks and hooligans that Duncan, or indeed anyone else, had ever seen collected together in one place. And they had all brought their knitting.

The silver tree next to a huge, well-muscled hooligan shook itself suddenly and started to play "The Bluebells of Scotland". The hooligan was so startled that he gave a little yelp and a pink bird that had been perched in the tree's branches took flight.

"Harriet made our trees," the young lady told Duncan. "Some of them light up," she added. "It's possible she made the birds as well, I'm not sure." The pink bird landed on the bald head of an evil looking thug with a picture of a razor blade tattooed on his neck. The thug said nothing, just continued to chew. The bird then hopped on to the shoulder of a ratty little villain in a sharp suit and sunglasses who bared his teeth in irritation. The bird pooed down his shoulder.

As Duncan was marched past the waiting villains nobody spoke, nobody smiled. The only one who seemed relaxed was a gent in a flat cap who was knitting and whistling a tune through his teeth. Mr Toffee Cheeseman was making himself a scarf and matching muffler for the winter.

"When you address Mrs Grunt you refer to her as 'marm' to rhyme with 'farm', rather than 'mam' to rhyme with 'spam'," the pale young lady told Duncan. She tapped on the door to Mrs Grunt's office, adjusting his hair to make him look more presentable while they waited for a reply. Duncan tried not to feel too miserable, after all what could Mrs Grunt actually do to him? She wasn't going to kill him, was she?

There, behind a huge desk made of pink marble, drinking tea from a china cup, little finger delicately raised, was Mrs Linoleum Grunt, Chairwoman of GrumpO Industries. She didn't say anything when she saw Duncan; she just let her teacup tremble in the air while she stared at him accusingly. Eventually Duncan could stand the silence no longer. Despite all the evidence of his short life he still believed that everybody would be reasonable if approached in the right way.

"Excuse me, Mrs Grunt," he began, "I think there must have been a misunderstanding."

"Despicable boy," she interrupted. "Vile worm of a boy. Nasty, loathsome, unhygienic little snake in the grass." She spoke slowly, precisely. "Sent here to spy on the project. I guessed what you were up to and ee-vents have proved me right." Duncan could feel his cheeks burning but he kept his head up. He looked her in the eye. "Ee-vents have been recorded, they have been spliced together. The evidence is damning and you will accept the consequences." She took a sip of her tea.

There was a tap on the door and the pale young lady returned. "Mr Crusher Bacon for you, marm."

Crusher Bacon shuffled in, carrying his knitting needles and ball of wool. He was the size of a small elephant and he had earrings in all sorts of places earrings shouldn't be. As she turned her attention from Duncan to the papers on her desk, Mrs Grunt's manner changed utterly.

"Mr Bacon, lovely to meet you, do sit down. I've been reviewing your application form, very impressive." He looked smug. "Although I always think it's more impressive," she continued, "if you don't get caught for robbing a bank than if you do." Crusher looked crestfallen for a moment but Mrs Grunt didn't pause for breath. "Obviously I can't say too much at this stage but my associates and I are involved in a project that will allow us to reach into nearly every family home. We want to put together a team of specialists, such as yourself, who can deal with the actual..." she chose her words carefully, "collecting! Do you see yourself as part of that team, Mr Bacon?"

Crusher, who had honestly not understood a great deal of what she had just said, tried to look evil and determined.

Why is she letting me hear all this? Duncan asked himself. The answer was not long in coming.

"Here is a question for you, Mr Bacon," purred Mrs Grunt. "We have here this unnecessary boy." She waved her hand in the direction of Duncan. "He's been poking around making a nuisance of himself. His silence must be guaranteed. How would you deal with that little problem?"

Crusher Bacon knitted his brows thoughtfully and studied Duncan.

"He 'ent very big," he observed at last.

"No, he's much too small," agreed Mrs Grunt.

After thinking for some considerable time Crusher added, "I'd heave him out the window."

Mrs Grunt did not reveal what she thought of this simple but effective solution, but she made a note.

It went on like this all morning. Duncan was Exhibit A in a series of job interviews. The kind of work was never spelt out, but he could see it was not going to involve helping old ladies across the road or comforting sick puppies.

Sharpy Malone, who still had bird poo down his jacket, came up with a very complicated solution which involved Duncan being kidnapped and taken on board a ship bound for the East Indies. Duncan recognised it as the plot of a film he had seen on TV. Mr Julian Peasemould, on the other hand, spent some time discussing poison, and how it might be offered to Duncan hidden inside various treats.

"Nice Victoria sponge, you'd like that, wouldn't you son?" He twisted around to grin at Duncan. "But what I recommend," he explained, "is putting the actual doins' in the jam. You don't want your doins' in the cake mix, cooking! Not good for it, see!"

"How interesting," commented Mrs Grunt dryly.

If Mrs Grunt had ever wondered why there was sometimes a dusting of grey powder on the rug in the middle of her office she had not bothered to investigate. Which was lucky because if she had she would have discovered a pencil inserted in a tiny hole next to the light fitting from the attic space above. Ursula's best den had a spyhole created by many hours of patient pencil waggling. That morning Ursula was laid out on her stomach in the dust watching Duncan and the parade of villains below. Duncan's precious phone was clasped in one hand. She had become Gizzmo in the world of Poo-Chi Planet and Gizzmo needed to keep the other Poo-Chi pets up to date with developments at Arthritis Hall.

Gizzmo says, "They say poison for Duncan."

RatboyRyan says, "You gotta rescue him."

Gizzmo says, "I know that but how to rescue?"

Ursula was actually starting to get a bit annoyed. What exactly was she supposed to do?

Gizzmo says, "One only of me here but many many them."

"The Honourable Jago Lumsden," announced a tall, elegant crook in a sleek suit. "Just parked the chopper on your roof, hope that's all right with one and all." He bowed low over Mrs Grunt's hand. "An honour," he murmured. "Such a reputation in our profession." He waved away her question about Duncan. "I never advise wasting time on children."

"Why would that be?" asked Mrs Grunt.

"They are so easy to discredit. Find some stolen goods in their bedroom, edit together some CCTV. Job done. No one will listen to a word they say."

Mrs Grunt smiled her lemony little smile.

"My thoughts exactly, Mr Lumsden."

"Call me Jago, dear lady, please!" And he kissed her hand again.

Jago was a great success. He told her marvellous tales of the terrible things he had done, some of which were even true, and after his interview had finished he did not leave. He stayed sprawled across her dainty furniture like a wicked giraffe, watching the proceedings with amused contempt.

Toffee, on the other hand, did not do well. He was polite enough: "How-djou-do?" he nodded to Jago. "How-djou-do, marm?" He even turned and nodded to Duncan. But it was downhill after that. When asked the Duncan question he couldn't seem to think of anything better than a good telling off. What he did want to explain was how to get the tension right for stocking stitch.

"You have to bring the wool round the back, see?" He held up his half-made muffler to show them how it should be done.

"Do buck up, Toffee," drawled Jago. "You're letting yourself down."

"Knitting was just a ruse, Mr Cheeseman," explained Mrs Grunt, not very patiently. "We are coming together for what some might consider a criminal con-speer-a-see. The knitting was just a pretence, a way of disguising our real intention."

Toffee was not to be put off so easily. "That's as maybe, I'm not disagreeing with you, but there's no denying the back of the work looks better if you keep an even tension."

There was a noise, like a hiss. It came from behind her. She swung round and stared into the blackness: nothing! She must remember that she, Ursula Meager, was never afraid of anything. She was not afraid of the dark, or the scuttling things that hid in it. There it was again, that noise. She felt sweat on her forehead. What if it was the monster?

Zhang says, "Maybe you make distraction so Duncan can get free."

RatboyRyan says, "Yeah or get weapon."

Messages flicked across the phone's little black screen, then dropped and dropped as the Poo-Chi pets kept their advice coming. Ursula wasn't looking. Here in the real world she was alone, and the monster was creeping towards her.

Meoww, complained Pork Pie. Ursula was overwhelmed with relief. She laughed, then sneezed, then laughed again. There was the baggy old cat crouched down, the hair on his back bristling, his one good eye gleaming at her, yellow and sour.

"It's OK," she told him. "I won't hurt you." Pork Pie sat back on his haunches. He was not afraid of the funny-smelling, sneezing girl thing. She was nothing. Ursula held out her fingers to the cat and made little kissing noises. Even if Pork Pie had been in a more relaxed and friendly mood, he still would not have understood what the kissing sound was supposed to mean, or what he was supposed to do about it. However, at that moment he was very far from relaxed. Every hair of his scabby old coat stood upright, every muscle tensed. There was something beyond the girl thing, something that frightened him very much indeed. He sensed its presence, felt it shift and flex. He hissed.

"It's all right," urged Ursula. But it wasn't all right, it was very far from all right.

Pork Pie sprang at the monster just as its arm began to swing. He became a spitting, biting, scratching ball of teeth and fur. As he leapt his claw sliced across Ursula's cheek. Not that she noticed. Even before her blood had time to spring into the fresh cut, the monster's cable-like arm whipped through the air, its three-pronged hand smashing against the side of her head. She was unconscious before she hit the ground.

You would have thought someone in Mrs Grunt's office would have noticed what was happening above their heads, but they didn't. Perhaps it was because the pale young lady receptionist had just burst in with some very exciting news.

"Miss Harriet says we are going to go today. She says you should come now." She couldn't resist an excited little clap of her hands.

The Honourable Jago Lumsden peeled himself off the couch and made a low bow to Mrs Grunt. "May I escort you, dear lady?"

Mrs Grunt glanced at Duncan, then at Toffee. "You! Watch the boy," she told Toffee. "I won't be long." She swept through the door marked *Operations Room* on Jago's arm.

It wasn't a very daring escape plan. It didn't involve any disguises or acts of ruthless violence. Duncan simply told Toffee that he needed the toilet and would be back in a minute. Toffee was so engrossed in a complicated bit of casting on that he didn't even look up. Duncan walked out of the office, through the waiting room, now luckily empty, and back to reception.

Keep calm, he told himself. *Look as if you're meant to be here*. He turned down a corridor marked *Utilities* to avoid a gaggle of technicians but they were heading for the Operations Room, too excited to worry about him.

The best thing would be to get out of here and tell someone what he had overheard, not that he was sure what that was. He stopped still and tried to think. He couldn't use the elevator because of all the cameras watching it. Looking around he noticed a caretaker's cupboard, and something else, something interesting. There was a small door or hatch without a handle, and he noticed that there was a ghost of a letter marked on it. The letter was A. In happier times the Armadillo Post must have extended all the way up to the top floor.

"You are going to have to put it on, Nathan, it's in your contract." It was a woman's voice and it was coming his way. There was no time. Duncan opened the door to the caretaker's cupboard and stepped in. Nathan and his minder, a woman from the talent agency, stopped to argue just outside.

"I'll look like a dork," Nathan yelled.

"No one will even know it's you."

"Well, why don't you wear it then?"

"Don't be silly."

It was very dark in the cupboard. It smelt of cleaning chemicals and old wet stuff.

"Look! You just have to wear it for half an hour," pleaded the woman. "Half an hour, Nathan! Wave, listen to a speech, then it's over. Don't you want Googley TV to be a success?"

"It's not like this is even the proper launch," moaned Nathan. "Who knows what those creeps are actually doing in there?"

The woman tried getting angry.

"Those creeps pay your fee, young man, and you would be well advised to remember that. Now do you want me to tell them that you want out of the contract? It will be expensive. You know a good lawyer, I assume."

There was rather a long, tense silence.

"Anyway," complained Nathan, "there isn't even anywhere to change."

The door to Duncan's cupboard was suddenly yanked open. He leant back, trying to disappear among the mops.

"Quickly," snapped the woman from the talent agency. "It starts in five minutes."

Nathan slouched in, followed by a huge pile of bright orange fur. The door was closed behind him and the cupboard was dark again. Nathan felt around until he found a box to sit on. Leaving the costume on the floor, he got out his phone and settled down with it. Duncan tried hard not to breathe.

"You better be getting changed," called Nathan's minder after a few minutes of silence. Nathan continued to tap at his screen, unconcerned.

"Nathan!" she snapped.

"Can't, can I?"

"Why not?"

"No light."

The door opened a couple of inches. Her hand felt around for the light switch, turned it on and withdrew.

The two boys looked at each other. It was an awkward situation and Duncan did not know what to say.

"Are you stalking me?" Nathan asked. Duncan shook his head. "Good. I'm always getting stalked."

"I'm hiding," explained Duncan.

"Good plan." Nathan turned his attention back to his screen. "I'm doing my blog," he said. "I'm saying I'm in a cupboard." After a while he added, "She thinks I'm wearing that stupid costume but I'm not looking like a dork for anyone."

Duncan had an idea. He heard the idea come out of his mouth before he'd had a chance to consider whether it was a good one or not, and as soon as he heard it he felt sure it was not.

"I'll wear it for you."

Nathan looked at him suspiciously for a long minute, eyes narrowed. He and Duncan were practically the same height.

"Yeah OK," he said. There was nothing else for it. Duncan climbed into the Googley suit. Nathan put the head on and turned him around to check that no part of Duncan was still visible under the bright orange fun fur.

"If anyone wants an autograph just say you've hurt your wrist," advised Nathan. "No, don't say anything. Don't speak at all."

Duncan nodded.

"Nathan!" The lady from the talent agency was really losing patience.

"Coming," called Nathan. He opened the door and pushed Duncan, dressed as a giant Googley, out to meet his fate.

"Quickly," she snapped. "We'll miss it." And she trotted off ahead while Duncan lumbered after her.

Mrs Grunt glared down at the crowd. A respectful silence fell.

-9-

IN WHICH URSULA IS TRAPPED,
DUNCAN IS STUBBORN
AND HARRIET GOES MISSING

URSULA CAME BACK to consciousness very suddenly, as if being yanked out of a deep dark place. There was banging in her head. There was a rhythm to the banging like hammer blows. Everything was wrong, everything hurt. The pain in her head and her limbs was so big there was no way to get beyond it.

She couldn't move. Her legs seemed to be held together by something. She could wriggle them a little, feel that they were bruised and achy, but she could not move them apart. Her arms too were pinned against her side. There was something across her face and sticking to her hair. Her mouth was covered. As she tried moving her jaw she could feel the tape pull at her skin.

Ursula wished very hard for this to be a bad dream. She wanted to go back to not feeling; not feeling was better. Inside her head she begged, *Please let me be by myself in my own newspaper bed.* But even as she prayed to be alone, she knew she wasn't. She could hear a busy scratchy sound somewhere close to her head but she could not turn to look. *Come on, Ursula, do something!*

She found she could move the fingers of her left hand, so slowly, cautiously, she felt around. The wrapping seemed to be tape, maybe parcel tape, the sort used by GrumpO Industries to package up all those boxes. She was wrapped, like an Egyptian mummy, in layers and layers of parcel tape.

Then suddenly something slammed against her side, making her gasp.

"Squeeze," said a thin metallic voice.

She was rolled over and then allowed to fall back as another strip of tape was wrapped around her chest. Poor Ursula, it hurt so much and she felt so frightened. She started to cry hopelessly. The wrapping was going to extend over her body until it covered her whole head and she would die of suffocation and no one would ever find her and her dad would be so sad and lonely without her.

Thinking about Mr Meager helped. He needed her, he wouldn't cope for a second on his own. The thought of his unhappiness made her try to control her panic. Cautiously Ursula tried to open her eyes.

One eye was covered in tape, it was stuck to her eyelid, but she could open the other eye a little.

At first she couldn't make out anything. The darkness seemed to wrap around her completely. But maybe it was not quite complete, there was some sort of blue light reflected on the ceiling. It seemed to grow, then die away and then grow again. What she could not see, because she could not move her head, was the thing right next to her. She held her breath and whatever it was seemed to pause too, as if it could sense her attention.

Then it lifted something up to show her, held it in front of her face. A three-pronged hand on the end of a long, cable-like arm was holding a package, about the length of her own leg but rounded at both ends. A package made of layers and layers of parcel tape.

"Squeeze," said the monster right next to her head. It closed the three metal fingers around the package and squeezed so that a thin, high wail of misery and despair rose from it.

"Mee... ee... eee... oo... www!" it cried hopelessly. It was Pork Pie inside all those wrappings. He had been wrapped up like a mummy while still alive.

"This is what I'm going to do to you," the monster seemed to be saying.

Ursula thought she might die of fright. She tensed every muscle and then shook herself ferociously, pushing and twisting against the layers that encased her. It didn't help much but there were some small victories. By throwing her head from side to side she managed to gain a little freedom of movement: she could at least turn her head. *Whack!* The monster slammed into her again. It didn't want her wiggling; wrapping a whole human, even if not a very big one, was hard enough without wiggling.

Do something, Ursula! Don't just lie there and let it cover you completely.

"Do yoo want sum juice?" she blurted out, her voice muffled by the tape across her mouth.

The monster did not respond.

"Yoo can have some juice if you wan," she added, trying to sound friendly and encouraging.

A yellow eye rose up on a cable beside her head. You might even think it was considering her question. Did it want some juice? There was a stillness while the blue light in the corner fizzed. Ursula could feel her heartbeats like hammer blows.

Suddenly the thing turned and scuttled off into the corner of the room with the blue glow. She could almost see it. It was big, like a bear or a washing machine, but low down to the ground. It moved like a huge insect scuttling on many legs. Its back was encased in a series of hard, overlapping strips. Ursula turned her head enough

to see it pick up a thick electric cable and drive the end
with the plug into its side. It was like a car putting the
nozzle from the petrol pump into its own petrol tank.
Maybe "juice" meant electricity? Maybe it was recharging.

Then the door in the corner eased open.

Great Aunt Harriet put her head round. She searched
out and found the monster and a look of sickening sop-
piness crept over her huge, horrible face.

"Don't worry, Fluffkin, it's only Mummy."

Working out what was going on in the Operations
Room from inside a Googley costume was harder than
Duncan had thought. He could tell there were lots of
people because they kept bumping into him. Some of
them slapped him on the back and cheered when they
saw him. Through the two eyeholes he could see Mrs
Linoleum Grunt standing above everyone else at a huge
lectern as if she was about to make an announcement
to the world's press.

It was the wall of screens behind Mrs Grunt that was
most amazing. There were rows and rows of screens,
maybe hundreds of them, and they were all turned
on. The whole world seemed to be pouring into that
room at the top of Arthritis Hall. Duncan didn't know

where to look first. Should he watch what was on telly in Afghanistan, or Fiji, or Moscow? Or look at a website, a war game, a blog, or a tweet? For a few seconds his attention was caught by a home video of a squirrel in a picnic basket singing a song about cheese. Then he noticed direct-feed CCTV for Arrivals at Dubai airport, Departures from Mumbai station.

Everywhere numbers were cascading down screens impossibly fast, calculating, measuring the flow of traffic through the Bering Strait, the price of chewing gum in every sweet shop averaged out to seventeen decimal places, the migration of sea cows and the number of comedy hats bought in Finland last Tuesday.

Mrs Grunt stepped onto a box to make sure everyone could see her. She rapped her pointer sharply on the lectern and glared down at the assembled technicians, electricians, engineers, assistants, marketing people, crooks, villains and thieves. A respectful silence fell.

There, on a screen in the corner, was a china rabbit lying on its side next to a cushion patterned with rabbits and a game of snakes and ladders. There was something oddly familiar about them. Duncan wondered why that screen caught his attention. After all, nothing was moving and the image was very gloomy. It was as if the camera had been dropped and forgotten, and the light turned off.

Mrs Grunt took out her pink glasses. She polished them carefully, checked them for smears and settled them delicately on her nose. Once she was comfortable she glared out at her audience.

"All you clever people," she sneered. A smirk of contempt escaped her on the word "clever" so that everyone felt ashamed, as if being clever was something bad. "As you know, today is the day that the project goes live. Today is the day we take on our biggest en-a-mee and destroy it. Today is the day we take the world of robotic pet substitutes by the throat and squeeze till we squeeze out every last drop of juice."

The word "juice" seemed to hang in the air in front of Duncan.

"Where is Mrs Pettigrew?" asked Mrs Grunt. Mrs Pettigrew turned out to be slumped on a chair next to the lectern, absorbed in her computer game. "Without Mrs Pettigrew's mathematical genius," Mrs Grunt told her audience, "this project could not have got off the ground. Thank you, Mrs Pettigrew, on behalf of GrumpO Industries." She led a round of applause which petered out nervously. Mrs Pettigrew ignored it.

"And Harriet, where are you?" There was silence as everyone looked around for Harriet. "Where is she?" Mrs Grunt snapped. She surveyed the room suspiciously as if accusing them all of concealing Harriet about their person. Someone brave at the back called out, "She just popped out for a bit."

Mrs Grunt went very still: she pursed her lips. Then she made a mental note. If she ever made a note like that about you, you would know that something very nasty was going to happen.

"This project is bigger than any one of us," insisted Mrs Grunt. "If Harriet has chosen not to be here on this special day she must take the consequences." She looked around as if daring her audience to argue with her; of course, nobody did. Mrs Grunt jabbed the toe of her pink shoe into the back of the technician in front of her, it was a signal to change the wall of screens. Duncan was startled to see every single one flip to Poo-Chi Planet.

Dear old Poo-Chi Planet. There it was, every lovely sky-blue-pink Poo-Chi pixel, the ice rink, the puzzle palace, the popsicle parlour, the emporium, the electric volcano disco and underwater ice hockey jamboree, and there was the candy-cane coloured moustache shop just where it should be. He felt a surge of longing; it all looked so happy and safe. He even thought he saw a familiar name flickering across one screen. It was Kobe, Duncan was almost sure. But what did Mrs Grunt want with Poo-Chi Planet?

"At noon today," explained Mrs Grunt, "Poo-Chi Planet will be annihilated. It will be as if it never existed."

What? Duncan was outraged. How could Poo-Chi Planet be an enemy? It made no sense. Mrs Grunt leant across the lectern and sneered.

"Just look at it," she urged. "Revolting! Isn't it?" Her audience mumbled, unsure what to say. "All those blue skies, all that fun!" The way she said "fun" made it sound like the most evil thing in the world. "It's got to go," she explained. "Too distracting. These children need to be buying Googleys, not having fun." Suddenly she smiled a big, pink, beaming smile. "It's for their own good."

Duncan considered pushing her off the stage. He could do it, he was only an arm's length away. His head was full of different ways of hurting Mrs Grunt when he heard her say, "But there are other en-a-mees of the project. In fact some of them are here in this room, now!" That made him pay attention. Her voice dropped to a low snarl. "Oh yes! Right here in this room. But believe me, they will be unmasked, they will take the consequences of their treachery! Which will be very nasty indeed." She smiled sourly at her audience.

The technician got another kick in the back and a huge clock face appeared in the middle of the Poo-Chi Planet screens.

"In a few moments Nathan will press the button for us. There will be a short celebration from twelve to twelve fifteen and then we will all return to our desks. This is where the hard work really begins." Mrs Linoleum Grunt rubbed her hands gleefully.

On one screen Duncan saw:

Kobe says, "He say all old girls gone. Now just Googleys."

Zhang says, "I believe there is danger to Gizzmo, we must watch."

"Nathan," called the woman from the talent agency.

He couldn't think how his friends on Poo-Chi Planet knew what was happening, but somehow they did.

"Nathan!"

People were turning to look at him, they held up their glasses of champagne and smiled encouragement. What did they want him to do? All at once he was grabbed, he was being hauled towards the stage. Of course, he was Nathan. And he was supposed to do something. He was pulled up to stand between Mrs Grunt and Mrs Pettigrew. The hands of the clock behind him trembled on the brink of noon. A countdown started: thirty-four, thirty-three, thirty-two. A big red button on a stand was placed in front of him.

Duncan looked back at the audience. He was now quite sure he was going to be discovered. Twenty-three, twenty-two, twenty-one... He would be discovered because he knew, with absolute certainty, that if pressing the red button meant destroying Poo-Chi Planet he could not do it. He would simply have to take his punishment whatever it turned out to be. He laced his fingers behind his back. Fifteen, fourteen, thirteen... He could see disaster coming but could do nothing to stop it. Nine, eight, seven... Glasses were raised. Five, four... He closed his eyes and waited for the worst to happen.

Now.

There was a horrible moment of silence. Everyone stared at him. It seemed to go on and on. Mrs Pettigrew looked up from her game, leant over and pressed the button.

"Slacker!" she hissed.

Grandma folded her arms and scowled, she had always known these computers would come to no good.

The number zero and the number one; I'm sure you knew about them before you even went to school. Everyone knows zero and one. They're very small, and very ordinary, but believe it or not they are what make computers work. Zero or one, yes or no, on or off.

A drop of water isn't much on its own, but enough of them together make an ocean and that has power, it can break the back of a ship or carry it from one continent to another. It's a bit like that with zero and one. Get enough of them together and start great strings of them shooting around the surface of the planet then things really start to happen! At noon on that day the huge string of zeros and ones, the code that made up the Poo-Chi Planet website, was captured by the signal sent from the top of Arthritis Hall. The zeros and ones were captured, kidnapped, throttled, ripped apart, and sent on their way as something different and something terrible.

On the other side of the world, at the point where one day ended and the next one began, there was very little immediate effect. On the northerly island of Ostrov Beringa, one child, who should have been asleep, was trying to log on to Poo-Chi Planet. He didn't get very far. His Poo-Chi pet told him: "Your prizes have been confiscated, your levels have been wiped out, your score is zero. Do not attempt to proceed." The message was repeated in a number of languages, none of which he understood. The boy clicked on his Poo-Chi pet a few times to see what would happen then he shrugged and went to look at a website about camels. It's best to be a relaxed sort of person if you live on Ostrov Beringa.

Other children didn't take the news so calmly. RatboyRyan was also supposed to be asleep.

"Your prizes have been confiscated, your levels have been wiped out, your score is zero. All access denied."

He couldn't believe it. He tried switching off and switching on again. He tried to bypass the log-in screen, nothing worked.

"Dad!" he yelled. "My computer's broken."

"Go to sleep!" Dad yelled back, not very sympathetically. RatboyRyan messaged his friends.

Children were outraged, crestfallen, anxious, angry, frustrated, enraged and baffled. How could such a thing happen? Beautiful Poo-Chi apartments, stuffed with trophies and prizes, could not be visited. Huge scores that had taken months to build up had been wiped out.

A lady who had a shop selling Poo-Chi jewellery usually had Poo-Chi Planet running live on thirty-eight screens. She was paralysed by indecision. She tried switching them all off but that seemed so final, so bleak. She switched them on again but the same announcement coming from thirty-eight speakers repeated over and over again in different languages made her feel crazy. In the end she stood in the middle of her shop and cried.

Zhang was supposed to be struggling with some knotty algebra when her Poo-Chi pet stopped working and just stared sadly back at her.

"Stop all that now and come and eat," Grandma told her.

"But all these equations," pleaded Zhang while she messaged Kobe to see if he knew what was going on. "Grandma, please let me solve them."

Grandma folded her arms and scowled, she had always known these computers would come to no good.

The number of people trying to log on to Poo-Chi Planet was even higher than usual. Everyone who heard the news wanted to check their own Poo-Chi. Reports of the calamity fizzed along wires and bounced off satellites. Websites for Poo-Chi fans crashed under the weight of traffic as people tried to figure out what had happened and how to get round it.

A farmer, who had Poo-Chi Planet playing all day because he believed his pigs liked it, kept trying to log on, each time hoping for a different result. In the end his best sow put her foot through his computer screen so he had to stop.

And what of Kobe?

"Your prizes have been confiscated, your levels have been wiped out, your score is zero. Do not attempt to proceed."

How had this happened? he asked himself. Then he asked himself, who had made this happen? If a bunch of zeros and ones start to behave oddly, it's not because they have taken it upon themselves to muck about. It's because someone has made them do it. Who might have altered the code for Poo-Chi Planet? Then

Kobe, in his father's office in Nairobi, asked himself if there was anything he could do about it. While his Poo-Chi pet stared back at him blankly from one screen, Kobe copied and saved the code streaming down the other.

It was early in the morning in Austin, Texas. The twins' mother came into their bedroom to wake them up. There was OboCurlyTops on the screen but she was different. She was not just hanging around waiting for the twins to play.

"Your prizes have been confiscated, your levels have been wiped out."

Mum sat down on the bed, horrified. What should she do? The twins loved Poo-Chi Planet. They would be so upset. Should she switch off the computer and risk alarming them by the sudden silence, the sudden absence of Poo-Chi? She had just decided to leave the computer on when the Poo-Chi pet OboCurlyTops stared out at the real world and said quite clearly, "You must never come back here. If you do I will tell everyone what you did!" All around the world the same message was repeated. "You must never come back here. If you do I will tell everyone what you did!"

How would you feel if someone threatened to tell the whole world what you did?

RatboyRyan thought about the time last Tuesday when he had kicked a boy who had beaten him in a swimming race. Kobe thought about taking his grandfather's watch apart to see how it worked and then not being able to put it back together and blaming his sister. Zhang hung her head and thought about all the times she'd lied to her grandma. It was a lot of times. She wondered how ashamed she really felt. She shrugged, a little ashamed maybe.

"A Googley is better," announced Poo-Chi Ratboy-Ryan. Flickering, losing his colour, he bowed to the watching world.

"Better get a Googley," said Poo-Chi OboCurlyTops as she faded into the deep black of the screen. "A Googley won't let you down," she promised, then blinked once, twice and was gone.

The twins in Austin, Texas, watched fascinated. They realised their mother was upset; she had been made very stressed and anxious by the whole thing. They were gentle, generous children so they fetched her a tissue and gave her a hug. When she finally stopped crying they asked, "So can we get a Googley?"

"Poor old Fluffkin," soothed Great Aunt Harriet, bending over the monster. "Mummy was getting worried, let's find you something nice to watch."

Now, thought Ursula, *now she's going to notice me.*

Harriet turned on a television and found a documentary about animals at a watering hole, setting it to repeat while she hummed tunelessly to herself. She pulled her phone out of a top pocket and held it up to her face. Her fingers flicked across the screen, checking and checking again. There was something on the phone that seemed to please her.

Maybe now, thought Ursula.

"All coming along very nicely." Harriet beamed at the monster in the corner. "Such a clever boy."

Things weren't coming along nicely as far as Ursula was concerned.

"Got to get back upstairs in a minute," Great Aunt Harriet told the monster, "Mummy's going to whack the internet today." She never could resist boasting. "Not breaking it, the internet that is, just giving it a good squeeze." Harriet drew out the word "squeeze" with horrible relish. She replaced her phone in her pocket so she had both hands free to demonstrate, twisting her huge fists around an imaginary throat.

"Squeeze," said the monster.

Harriet was delighted. She clapped her hands. "Aren't you a clever Fluffkin! Mummy's special boy."

Ursula thought she might be sick.

"ID'S NOT A HE!" she yelled from inside her cocoon of tape.

Great Aunt Harriet swung around.

"Id's not a he, id's a id!" repeated Ursula.

It would almost have been funny, the way the colour drained from Harriet's face as she realised the voice was coming from that huge, untidy lump of parcel tape. The idea that her Fluffkin might be responsible crystallised for a second in Harriet's fizzing brain before immediately disintegrating again; no, not her Fluffkin, it was impossible.

"'Elp me!" demanded Ursula.

"Shh," ordered Harriet, "he doesn't like shouting."

"'E doesn't like shouting, doesn't 'e?" shouted Ursula.

The monster still squatted in the corner with its eyes shut, glowing slightly blue.

"You must have made him cross," insisted Harriet. She was getting cross herself.

"Me! Dis is my fault, is it?"

Who knows how long they would have carried on arguing if something much more dramatic had not happened. It was, at that moment, precisely nine seconds after noon, the exact time Mrs Pettigrew pressed the button on the top floor of Arthritis Hall.

Any adult will tell you that too much electricity is a very dangerous thing. Not just a bit bothersome, or slightly worrying, or quite annoying, but properly, blisteringly disastrous. And this wasn't just a bit too much electricity, it was very much too much.

The monster was still plugged into the electricity supply when, at nine seconds after noon, a vivid blue flash ripped through its body and out across the room.

Harriet was knocked off her feet but Ursula was mostly insulated from the shock by the many many layers of tape wrapped around her. It was the monster that took the full force. It screamed. It was a horrible, high-pitched wail of agony.

Neither Harriet nor Ursula actually saw what happened next. Harriet had been knocked unconscious and Ursula simply closed her eyes. She couldn't help herself. For a minute and a half the monster absorbed enough electricity to run a small city. Juice came pouring in, filling it up, bloating it, then stretching it. It screamed as every nerve and fibre, every wire and connection that held it together, expanded. It was growing so fast it felt like it was bursting.

Mrs Grunt pulled the head off Duncan's Googley costume.

"I knew it!" she shrieked. "A sneak thief, a spy."

Everyone stared and, despite himself, Duncan blushed, which, of course, made him look guilty.

"A delinquent," roared Mrs Grunt. "A reprobate, an en-a-mee, a trespasser, a liar, a burglar, a kidnapper!"

"How am I a kidnapper?" he mumbled because he had to try and defend himself somehow.

"How am I a kidnapper?" repeated Mrs Grunt so that everyone in the Operations Room, and quite a lot beyond, could hear. "Where is Nathan?" she asked. "Tied up somewhere, I suppose. And Harriet? What have you done with her?" The audience began to mutter. It was true no one had seen Harriet for some time. "One of your prisoners no doubt. What about Ursula?" As the charges against Duncan piled up the crowd got angrier. Mrs Grunt dropped her voice to a vicious hiss. "Not too sure about Ursula are you, boy? Thought she wasn't quite clever enough for you! Is that what you told Poo-Chi Zh-ang?" She dragged out each syllable, grinning like a wolf who smells its dinner. "Or RatboyRyan, now isn't he a charmer!" Duncan suddenly wanted to cry, though of course he didn't. He felt as though Mrs Grunt had climbed inside his head and poisoned everything she found there.

"It's the ingratitude that's so hard to bear," Mrs Grunt complained to everyone, as if Duncan had rejected her many acts of kindness. "I blame myself, I let him worm his way in here." As ever with Mrs Grunt, it was impossible to know if she believed what she was saying or was just playing a part. She pointed to the Honourable Jago Lumsden and Crusher Bacon. "Take him to my office, I can't bear to look at him," she told them. "I will deal with him later."

After being hauled out of his bright orange fur suit, Duncan was held by each arm and forced to lumber along between Jago and Crusher. He hated the way people looked at him, the stares of anger and contempt. He knew he was blushing and hated himself for doing it.

"Shall we tie him up?" asked Crusher once they reached Mrs Grunt's office. Toffee, who had been happily settled in one of Mrs Grunt's armchairs getting on with his knitting, looked at Duncan with some concern.

"You were a long time on the lavvy, weren't you, son?"

"Toffee, old chap," drawled Jago. "Weren't you supposed to be watching this young hooligan?"

Toffee shrugged. "What's he done then?"

"Been unmasked as a spy."

"A spy!" Crusher was excited, he cracked his knuckles menacingly.

"A spy," Jago repeated with some satisfaction. "Out to destroy the dear lady's project."

"I'm not a spy," Duncan pointed out reasonably. No one paid him any attention.

"He's probably done away with the lad who should be here today," continued Jago. "Probably working for the police. He's aiming to let his chums in here and arrest us all."

Crusher was outraged! "They better not arrest me. I'm getting married next week." He had been told there would be a chocolate fountain at the wedding reception and he'd been really looking forward to it. "Shall I bash him up?" he asked.

"I suppose it might loosen his tongue," Jago mused.

Crusher flexed his shoulders in anticipation. The mere sight of Crusher's huge bulk, his tattoos and metal rings, was too much for Duncan.

"I'm not a police spy," he said rather desperately. "I'm a child. How could I be working for the police? They don't employ children."

"Lad's got a point," said Toffee.

"Yeah," said Crusher.

"Besides," added Duncan, "there's nothing criminal going on here, they're just selling toys, why would the police bother about that?"

"Just toys," Jago sneered. "It's never *just* anything with the dear lady, she's a criminal genius. A true star. If she wants to get those nasty-looking Googley articles into every home there will be a good reason. You can depend on that."

A Googley in every home, even, it seemed, in Ursula's home. Why would the horrible Mrs Grunt, who never did anything nice, give Ursula a Googley? Duncan remembered being under Ursula's table. He remembered the buttery warm glow, the cushion embroidered with rabbits, the china rabbit, the game of snakes and ladders taken from Daisy's apartment. There was something at the back of his mind, something that he needed to pay attention to.

"Why would she bother to get professionals like ourselves involved," drawled Jago, "if she was just selling toys?"

"Yeah," agreed Crusher.

There it was, finally, crystal clear. The screen he had noticed in the corner of the Operations Room, the one showing a china rabbit lying on its side next to a cushion patterned with rabbits and a game of snakes and ladders. All things that Ursula had taken from Daisy's apartment and kept in her own under-the-table den. That screen was showing the view under the Meagers' table, and where was the camera that was recording that view? It must be inside her brand-new birthday Googley. Where else could it possibly be? A present Mrs Grunt had given her so she could spy on her any time she chose. That's how he had been caught. Mrs Grunt had been watching them all the time through the eyes of a Googley.

"Is he gonna tell on us?" Crusher asked, nodding in Duncan's direction.

"I expect he is, old chum," Jago replied.

"Shall I shut him up then?"

"Probably should."

As Crusher advanced towards him, rolling up his sleeves so he could get down to some serious work, Duncan opened his mouth and hoped something helpful would come out.

"I don't work for the police," he said. "I work for someone else. They'll pay a ransom for me, probably."

"How much?" Crusher leant over him, showing him two huge fists. He had the word "narked" tattooed across his knuckles but written as $KNARRKED$, which is not even spelt right. Duncan thought he'd better not point this out.

"And who?" added Jago.

"Poo-Chi Planet," confessed Duncan.

"Ahh," beamed Jago. "The commercial rival!" He preened. "I thought so."

"Yes," said Duncan. "I have to let the attack force from Poo-Chi Planet in here tonight. We organised it through the website." Hopefully Jago and Crusher had never actually seen Poo-Chi Planet. While he talked his brain raced ahead. "There's a secret system of tunnels running through the building. They were put there by the Poo-Chi Planet people. It was a couple of months ago, we knew something was going on here. We have code names, you see. I'm called Gizzmo and there's Zhang, Mrs Grunt knows about Zhang."

Where had that come from? Duncan wondered. It sounded ridiculous to him but at least two out of the three villains seemed to be drinking it in. "They're marked with an 'A', the tunnels, A for..." He searched his brain desperately. *Not aardvark*, he told himself. But when you are trying not to think about aardvarks somehow they keep intruding. "Advanced espionage network," he said at last, thinking it sounded rather stupid.

"Sounds like a story to me," said Toffee.

"I can show you if you want," Duncan offered.

"He might be trying to get away," pointed out Crusher, who then could not help showing how very pleased with himself he felt for seeing the danger.

"How could I get away from all three of you?" Duncan asked. "You're three grown men and I am one child."

That was how Toffee, Jago, Crusher and Duncan came to be in the Utilities corridor examining the mysterious panel marked with an "A".

"Bit old, isn't it, been here for ages I would have thought," said Toffee.

"They do that on purpose," explained Duncan. "To make it blend in, they have a team doing it. They come in disguised as painters and decorators, they go to a special college to learn how to do it."

Toffee gave him a long hard look.

Don't get carried away, Duncan told himself.

"Let's get it open," said Jago. "Have a look-see."

They prised off the small door and, sure enough, there was a tunnel at floor level about a foot and a half high. They all got down on their hands and knees to examine it better. It was too dark to see much.

"Here," said Toffee. He got out a torch and shone it into the tunnel.

"They're very well made," Duncan explained. "Look, I'll show you." He took the torch from Toffee and eased himself into the tunnel. Propped up on one elbow he shone the light on the side walls, pointing out a few points of interest.

"They have specially made tools to get this effect," he told them.

Jago and Crusher nodded.

"But further back here..." Duncan pulled himself a couple of feet further in.

He kept talking about little Poo-Chi tunnel builders and their special tools and their instructors and their top-secret training courses. He made another move deeper in.

"Ingenious," mused Jago, his chin in his hand.

It had, of course, occurred to Duncan, as it will have occurred to you, that there was one place where being a smallish child, instead of three large adults, was a real advantage. He allowed himself a smile.

"Well grab him, you idiot," yelled Jago, suddenly realising what Duncan was up to.

Crusher reached after Duncan but he was too far in and Crusher was much too big to follow. As Duncan crawled away he could hear Jago and Crusher cursing and blaming each other and swearing to get even.

Duncan still hated these confined spaces but he knew the trick of not being scared is to concentrate on the next thing that has to be done and not let your imagination run away with you.

webs, dead insects and bat poo covered everything. He focused the torch more carefully. No, not quite everything. It looked as if something heavy had been dragged through the dirt. He felt suddenly cold. What could have made that trail? He didn't want it to be Ursula; he found he did not want anything bad to have happened to her. Duncan put his phone in his back pocket, Toffee's torch between his teeth, and set off crawling along the rafters to follow the trail.

He still hated these confined spaces but he knew the trick of not being scared is to concentrate on the next thing that has to be done and not let your imagination run away with you. He ignored the infinite dark pressing around him, the scuttling things, the wheezing and burping of the pipes. He ignored the splinters in his hands and his cut knees. It was harder to ignore the memory of the monster from Daisy's apartment. In particular the way it had grabbed poor Ursula round the throat. That was the thought that must be ignored most of all.

He tried to concentrate on following the trail, sometimes it was faint, sometimes very clear. It led down from the top floor, through hatches, through the backs of broom cupboards, at one point out along the fire escape. It got harder to follow once it left the attics but Duncan could still see signs of something heavy being squeezed and dragged along. He was also starting to pick out a sound above the clatter of the pipes and the elevator. A voice, steady and calm. As he dropped down into another part of the tunnel on the floor below it was suddenly sharper. He could make out the words.

"These huge beasts have hardly changed since the age of the dinosaurs. They have a well-earned reputation as heartless killers."

Duncan felt sick. The voice he could hear was coming from a television and he could guess where that television was. He had spent enough time in Great Aunt Harriet's box room listening to nature programmes to be in no doubt.

"Though they can grow to be huge – the length of a London bus is not uncommon – they move with great agility when catching their prey." This was followed by splashing and shrieking as whatever was being described brought down an elk, or an elephant, or an ice-cream van.

The torch showed the trail ahead of him veer off down a side tunnel. He crept near enough to look around the corner and flash the torch to see where it went. In fact it was not a tunnel; he was facing a closed doorway. On the other side of the door the television continued to describe what a crocodile was doing to the leg of an okapi. The trail was clear, whatever had been dragged along this tunnel had been dragged through that doorway into Harriet's apartment and the door shut after it.

Of course it might not be Ursula. Just because he couldn't think of another explanation didn't mean there wasn't one. Maybe it was a giant ferret pulling a bin bag full of love letters, or an industrial vacuum cleaner with a dead sheep caught in its cables. Maybe, but probably not. Here he was at the back of Harriet's locked room. The one she had erupted out of on the day he first arrived. There was a good chance that Ursula was in there with the monster from Daisy's apartment; and he, Duncan, was going to have to try and rescue her. Generally he got good marks at school for English, maths and science. He would have got quite good marks for "keeping your head in a crisis" if such a lesson existed; but fighting monsters, that was never going to be his best subject. And here, crouched in the dark with nothing but a torch, he really wished he didn't have to try.

The door in front of him turned out to be really odd. It was made of two or three overlapping sections that seemed to be bulging out at him and then falling away at the floor. He reached out and touched it; his finger recoiled from the unexpectedly warm surface.

"Ursula," he whispered. "Are you in there?"

There was no answer. He was going to feel so silly if he had got this wrong.

"Ursula?" He raised his voice a little. Still nothing.

"I'm no good at this," he complained to himself out loud. "Anybody would do better at this. I'm too short, I'm scared of everything and I'm no good at games." Unfortunately there was no one else. If that door needed to be smashed open he would have to be the one to do it.

He twisted round in the tunnel so that he could extend his legs. Then, bracing himself against the walls, he put both feet against the door and shoved. There was a high-pitched howl of indignation from inside and the door moved. It moved but not as he had expected. It didn't fall forward or swing open, it gave a little and then slid across, pulled away from the doorway and then settled again.

Duncan had thought he might have to deal with a monster on the other side of the door. A horrible suspicion was beginning to form that somehow the monster *was* the door. But surely that wasn't possible. Any monster able to move about in these tunnels was much too small to cover the entire doorway. Every time he thought he couldn't get more frightened he found out that he could.

Now the thing in front of him had moved there was something showing on the floor. The end of a piece of parcel tape. Without thinking too hard, because thinking just seemed to make things worse, Duncan grabbed the tape and yanked. At first nothing happened so he yanked again, harder.

There was a muffled groan from somewhere in the room then the bulk in front of him shifted again.

"Squeeze," screamed the monster, outraged.

Duncan would one day think of what happened next as the battle of Harriet's back bedroom. That is perhaps a bit too grand but there's no doubt it was a proper fight. He used his feet, kicking and kicking, yanking on the tape at the same time. The monster shifted, screaming, bashing about inside until it freed a huge metallic arm and shoved it back into the tunnel. It swung viciously at Duncan, who just about managed to protect his head from being smashed against the wall but got a real whack on the arm.

"Squeeze!" screamed the monster.

"Squeeze you," yelled Duncan. He let the torch fall and grabbed the swinging arm. Its three-pronged hand was opening and closing, trying to clutch at him. He stamped on it with all his strength, grinding it against the wall.

"Squeezeeeeeeeeeeeeeeeeeeeee... e... e..." came the scream again.

There was the torch at his feet. Duncan grabbed the edge of one piece of the monster's armour. He put his foot on the piece below and pressed down, opening a space between the two plates. Then he picked up the torch and shoved it, as hard as he could, into the gap.

"Squeezeee... eee... e... eee..."

Duncan kicked the end of the torch, driving it in further, like a hammer driving a nail into flesh.

Beyond the screaming and the television there was a tremendous noise. More than the monster trying to turn, knocking things flying as it twisted round. The noise felt like one giant roar of destruction. An eruption or earthquake. It felt like everything was being smashed as it came clattering down around him. Duncan covered his head and shut his eyes and waited to die. The return of stillness took him by surprise. He took a breath and opened his eyes.

The world was now entirely different. The monster was gone and the darkness had gone. In front of him was a cloud of dust lit by a new light from the room beyond. The dust seemed to shimmer and hang in the air thoughtfully, as if it was just as surprised to be there as Duncan was to see it. The television, now on its back, was still talking.

Perhaps because he had arrived here from a strange place and was looking from an odd angle, perhaps because the arrangement of walls and door that had made up Harriet's apartment had been totally destroyed, it took Duncan more than a few seconds to realise what he was looking at. It wasn't just that the door labelled on the other side with a _No Entry_ sign in green ink had gone, almost all of the wall that it had been part of was gone too. He could see the fine mist of brick dust settling on the glorious mess of what had been Harriet's front room. The tuba and bicycle and washing machines, the benches and bell jars were still visible among the rubble. It was as if a bus had been driven, not very carefully, through Great Aunt Harriet's apartment.

Was that a cough? He thought he heard something.

There was a body lying sprawled face down in the dust. _Great Aunt Harriet, was she dead?_ She looked dead.

"Stot her!"

Stupidly Duncan stared at the back of Great Aunt Harriet's head. Was she speaking to him?

"Stot her! She miyd get away!" It was a strange muffled voice, it sounded like it was coming from under several blankets.

"Who might get away?" he asked out loud.

"Harriet, od cors."

The voice was clearly very frustrated. "Cun an get her, stot her."

"Stot her?" Duncan repeated.

Suddenly there was Mr Meager on the other side, where Harriet's wall should be. He stared at Duncan, ashen-faced.

"I heard a noise," he said.

"Yes," replied Duncan. It seemed impossible that anyone could not have heard the wreckage of Harriet's apartment.

"I heard a noise so I came to see."

They stared at each other for a moment. Mr Meager was obviously struggling to understand how Duncan, one short boy, had caused all this destruction. Duncan, meanwhile, was facing up to the impossibility of explaining how it was not really him that had pushed whole walls down but a huge armoured monster.

"Dad! Dad!"

"Ursula?" Mr Meager looked around wildly. "Where are you?"

"'Ere, I'm 'ere." Finally Duncan and Mr Meager understood that the great mass of parcel tape, now covered in brick dust, that had been squished and flattened against the wall, contained Ursula. They scrabbled at the tape with their hands, pulling it away from her face.

"Ursula, gawd help us, what have they done to you?" cried Mr Meager. She tried to speak but started to cough as she inhaled dust. She looked terrible, her face was streaked with tears and snot and scratches.

"All right, petal, we got you, you're all right now," soothed Mr Meager, cradling the cocoon of tape that contained his daughter. Duncan got her some water and they held it up to her lips. It seemed to help.

"Stop her!" Ursula shouted at Duncan once she could speak again.

"Who?"

"Harriet!"

Duncan had forgotten about Harriet, but, to please Ursula, he went and checked his sprawled, dusty, silent great aunt. The thought that all this was going to be very hard to explain kept reoccurring like a nagging toothache.

"Stop her running away, it's all her fault," insisted Ursula. In case Harriet wasn't dead he found some tape and wrapped it around her wrists, pinning them together behind her back. Then he and Mr Meager worked to free Ursula. She cried most of the time, partly because she had been so frightened, partly because her limbs were so stiff, and hurt so much when she tried to move them.

"Who did this to my girl?" asked Mr Meager. "Who wrapped her up? They want seeing to, it's not right." Normally he was not a man to make a fuss but he felt, in this case, he was owed an explanation.

Duncan and Ursula together tried to describe what they had seen. They told Mr Meager about a monster made of hard, interlocking sections, like a giant woodlouse. They described its many legs, six arms, and horrible, squeezing, three-pronged hands. They found it hard to agree on the size because nothing about its size made any sense.

As I am sure you know, when a child tells an adult important news, like Grandma is an international jewel thief, or aliens are eating the toothpaste, the adult might laugh, or sigh, or simply go on watching the television. What they won't do is spring into action. Duncan knew how it sounded. They were children telling an adult about a monster that stalked them through tunnels, sucked up electricity and turned people into living cocoons. He wouldn't believe it himself. He looked around for something to back up his story.

"It looks like that," Duncan pointed at a drawing on Great Aunt Harriet's wall, "but there must be more than one because Ursula and I got attacked the other day and that one was much smaller."

"Just one," insisted Ursula quietly. "There was a blue flash and that thing started to grow, it grew incredibly fast. It was screaming. It got so big it nearly squashed me completely. It nearly broke the room apart." Being squashed against the wall by a screaming, writhing, expanding monster, waiting for her bones to break and her last breath to be flattened out of her, was just about the nastiest thing that had ever happened to Ursula. She shrugged and gave a little laugh although it obviously wasn't funny. Mr Meager put an arm around her.

"And she calls it Fluffkin!" added Ursula.

"Who does?"

"Harriet, she thinks it's her pet or something."

Duncan and Mr Meager stared at her.

"Fluffkin?"

"It's her fault, she shouldn't let it hurt people." Ursula suddenly felt really angry. "If it's her monster she should make it behave."

Harriet gave a moan like air coming out of an old paddling pool. So not dead then.

Duncan fetched some water and dripped it into her mouth. The results were dramatic. She retched and gagged and spluttered; and then, discovering that her hands were pinned behind her back, she began to curse and gyrate, throwing herself back and forward in a jackknife motion.

Duncan watched this pantomime but without really seeing it. He looked again at the drawings on the wall. Drawings that, presumably, Harriet had made on her own wall. *Had she made them to record the monster? Or had she*, and Duncan couldn't quite get the thought organised in his head it seemed so bizarre, *made them to work out its design?* Now he looked properly he could see parts of the monster. There was the three-pronged hand; there was a diagram to show the wiring to its brain. And there, woven in and around the diagrams of its working parts, was a drawing of a Googley.

"Is it an animal?" he asked, quite conversationally.

"What do you mean, son?" said Mr Meager.

"The monster, is it an animal? It's not an animal, is it?" Duncan answered his own question.

"Can't be," replied Ursula.

"But it behaves like an animal."

"Maybe it's a robot?" suggested Ursula.

"Can't be a robot if it can grow," Duncan replied.

Ursula considered this.

"Maybe it's some kind of Googley?"

Harriet could restrain herself no longer. "Don't be ridiculous, idiot girl!" she fumed. "Those stupid Googleys, they're just a surveillance device, a camera and a computer wrapped up in a bit of fun fur. Of course I made Fluffkin. I'm his mummy." With relief Harriet gave up the huge effort involved in not boasting. "I could explain how remarkable he is, right on the cutting edge of organic robotic technology, but would it be worth it?

You're all much too dense to understand. Like a Googley indeed!" It seemed this was the single most upsetting idea Harriet had ever come across.

"I bet you made them though, those stupid Googleys," Ursula accused her.

"Well obviously!" retorted Harriet. "But they're for Linoleum, they're her project, from the engineering point of view they are of no interest whatsoever. Fluffkin, you see, he doesn't just copy, he can learn and develop. A new robotic life form that can adapt to changing physical circumstances. He's a world-class project, I'm expecting a Nobel Prize."

Duncan was bemused. "But you'd have to be really really clever to make a robot that could grow."

"Me! I'm that clever actually, me and Pettigrew, she wrote the software, we're more intelligent, pound for pound, than any other human beings on the planet."

"Does changing physical circumstances mean growing?" asked Duncan.

"Obviously, nin-com-poop!" Harriet told him. "Every time he plugs in for a recharge he is programmed to grow by 0.5%. It presented some very interesting challenges mechanically speaking. Not that you'd understand."

"So when it's plugged in to the electricity supply it's programmed to grow a certain amount?" Duncan checked that he had understood.

"I just said that, didn't I!" snapped Harriet.

"But it grew a lot more than that today."

"There was a surge in the electricity earlier," remembered Mr Meager. "It blew my fuses out."

"Yes, of course there was an electrical surge. I had actually organised that there should be. It was necessary for... business upstairs." Harriet went pale and then bright red then pale again as she looked around and considered the evidence with her own eyes. "I just didn't think... I didn't think he'd be recharging at that exact time... Maybe a slight malfunction of the software, a minor setback. You can untie me now, I have things to do. Linoleum needs me upstairs and Fluffkin won't like being out there on his own."

"No, we're not going to untie you actually," Ursula raged at her. "We're never going to untie you. You'll just have to lie there for ever and wee in your pants."

Harriet made a noise of rage like a furious foghorn.

"And," said Ursula, "we're going to get the army to blow up that thing. It's dangerous and it's got a stupid name."

Mr Meager, Duncan and Ursula put their hands over their ears while Harriet raged and cursed. She was being kidnapped and held prisoner against her will, Fluffkin was simply high-spirited and playful. Like all young people they were obsessed with health and safety; and, if they didn't release her immediately, Linoleum would sort them all out, in truly nasty ways.

This last threat obviously made Mr Meager nervous. He looked at his daughter. *Maybe we should untie her*, he seemed to suggest. She glared back at him. As a kind of compromise, Duncan and Mr Meager carefully picked Harriet up from the ground and pulled her to a sitting position, but they did not untie her hands.

"That thing, whatever it is, the thing she made," insisted Ursula, "it wrapped me up in tape like a mummy or something." She badly wanted Duncan and her father to understand how upsetting it had been. "If you hadn't come along what would have happened? What was it going to do to me next?"

Duncan remembered something from his very first night in Arthritis Hall: the nature documentary that had repeated over and over again, the one with the spider catching its prey and wrapping it up like a cocoon. That must have been for Fluffkin's benefit.

"So it wraps up its prey like a spider?" Duncan suggested. Harriet arched her eyebrows and pursed her lips, making a pantomime of not replying. "And," continued Duncan, "it squeezes them like a Peruvian mole!"

"Could he learn behaviour from the television, that was the question, and *voilà*! We can only deduce that he can." Harriet sneered as if here was more evidence of her vastly superior brain. "Nature documentaries! I thought they might be the thing!"

"So what's it been watching recently?" demanded Ursula. It was a very good question and they did not have to look far for the answer. The television, still on its back, was showing a huge crocodile, with the remains of an okapi flapping about between its jaws.

*Ursula found an old school tie and tied the pigeon
in place, finishing with a big floppy bow.*

-12-

IN WHICH EVERYTHING GOES
FROM BAD TO WORSE

WHEN FLUFFKIN burst out of Harriet's apartment the sound of the destruction was heard all the way up on the top floor. The queue of villains and burglars hoping to become part of Mrs Grunt's knitting circle looked at each other. Sharpy Malone sucked his teeth and shook his head. Maybe someone was blowing up a safe somewhere.

"Sloppy," he said to no one in particular.

"Indeed," replied Jago, but just then the pale young lady receptionist bustled up. She handed each of them a label on a long ribbon to hang around their neck. It showed their name followed by "GrumpO Industries, delegate". Crusher Bacon liked the idea of being a delegate though he wasn't quite sure what one was. Then the door to the Operations Room was opened and they were shooed inside. The party had been entirely cleared away; the technicians were back at their workstations and a ring of chairs, several rows deep, had been arranged in front of the lectern.

"There are briefing notes on your chairs," the receptionist said to the air above their heads. "Mrs Grunt's presentation will begin in precisely four minutes and there will be a test later."

On the back row Jago and Crusher were crestfallen. Mrs Grunt hadn't been too pleased that they'd let Duncan slip through their fingers. Ground was going to have to be made up. Toffee, on the other hand, was thinking about technical matters like whether to experiment with four ply or chunky.

Most of the burglars and villains watched the screens on the huge wall behind the lectern, though there wasn't much to see. Some were showing Googley TV; the rest showed bedrooms, kitchens, hallways, the inside of a bag, or a locker, or a car. Nothing much seemed to be going on. Occasionally a child, or a dog, or a vacuum cleaner moved in front of the camera. On one screen a little girl was gazing into the camera and singing a song about worms. The villains shifted in their seats, they were getting bored and that made them sullen; they started to chat and grumble. But when Mrs Linoleum Grunt, pert in pink from top to toe, click-clacked into the room they all fell silent. As she arranged her glasses on the end of her little pink nose and scowled down at them from the lectern they looked at the floor. Like the worst class in the school meeting the headmistress from hell, they knew that they had met their match.

"So, there is a monster, designed and made by Great Aunt Harriet, on the loose somewhere in Arthritis Hall," Duncan explained to Ursula and her father who, in fact, already knew. "This thing, whatever it's called..." he couldn't bring himself to say "Fluffkin" out loud, it was too embarrassing, "wants to grab people and wrap them up. It's an awful lot bigger than it thinks it is. It also thinks it's a crocodile which is not that helpful. I suppose we need to decide what to do about it."

Mr Meager nodded sagely but didn't suggest a plan.

Duncan imagined, for a second, a group of uniformed officers putting a blanket round his shoulders and handing him a comforting mug of cocoa.

"You've done a great job, son," they would say, "we'll take it from here."

In his experience grown-ups always acted like they were in charge until you actually needed them to be in charge and then they were always doing something else, something pointless like hoovering, or pebble-dashing the shed.

"We could take a vote," suggested Ursula. "I vote we get the police to blow the whole place up."

"Maybe we should try and warn people first," said Duncan. He was actually thinking about Toffee Cheeseman when he said this. The other people on the top floor of Arthritis Hall had mostly been unpleasant and if they got whacked by a demented robot he was not sure he minded too much. But what about Toffee? He had said good morning, and smiled and whistled companionably through his teeth while he knitted. There are some people in the world who can tell the difference between what they want to do and what they should do. Unfortunately for him, Duncan was one of these. He shrugged. "I think we should at least try."

There was no use appealing to Great Aunt Harriet for help—she was obviously going to make things as difficult as she could. She had retreated into silence, her vast nose in the air and the expression of a misunderstood saint on her horrible features, but she couldn't keep it up. She was not good at being quiet.

"Fluffkin is not naturally violent. He would never behave like that," she grumbled. "You and that girl must have smashed up my apartment deliberately." To show which girl she meant, Harriet threw a look of bitterness and contempt at Ursula.

"I punched myself in the face and then wrapped myself up in layers of tape, did I?" demanded Ursula furiously. She bared her arms which were crisscrossed with red marks, her tummy and back were scratched and bruised.

"Well I think you're very vicious children," complained Harriet. "I don't know why you won't leave Fluffkin alone."

"It could hurt people," explained Duncan steadily. "It's maybe not a good idea to have it charging about the place bashing down walls, grabbing people."

"Lad's got a point," Mr Meager added, trying to be helpful.

"This is not your business, Meager," snapped Harriet. "You insufferable little non-entity, why don't you get back to your sweeping or whatever you do." Mr Meager blushed and looked at the floor. Ursula, however, went white with rage.

Her revenge was swift and silent. She dragged over a tuba from what had been Harriet's front room. Harriet's already tied hands, their long knobbly fingers twisting in fury, were then tied, with more tape, to the tuba. Ursula then found a broom, a broken golfing umbrella, a long bow and a set of bellows which she inserted between the tuba and Great Aunt Harriet's back as if they were part of a huge flower arrangement. Her best find was a stuffed, cross-eyed pigeon from under Harriet's work-bench. This was perched, jauntily, on top of Harriet's head like a cherry on a fairy cake. Harriet gnashed her teeth in fury and shook her head to try and dislodge it, so Ursula found an old school tie and tied the pigeon in place, finishing with a big floppy bow. She stood back to admire the effect. Yes, she was pleased with her handiwork. Ignoring Harriet's bitter protests she removed her mobile phone from her top pocket and took a picture with it.

"How do I put this on the internet?" she asked, showing Duncan the photograph on Harriet's phone.

"Look for a browser." Duncan didn't like to say so but he thought they had more important things to worry about than uploading photographs. Ursula tried pressing a variety of buttons before giving up and handing it to Duncan in bewilderment.

"It says 'Present Iris', who's Iris?"

"It's locked," Duncan explained. "It means take a photo of your eye to unlock it."

"My eye?" she asked.

"No, hers."

"Oh yes, I saw her do that, I saw her hold it up to her eye and then check stuff on the phone."

"What stuff?"

"Don't know, about the monster I think." A thought occurred to her. "That could be useful maybe?"

"Yes," agreed Duncan, "it could be."

What followed was a very undignified and noisy scramble in which Mr Meager held Harriet's head still while Ursula, kneeling on her legs, prised open her tightly shut eyelids and Duncan held up her phone. Harriet cursed and threatened; she looked wildly from side to side, she tried to roll her eyes up into her head, which is a horrible thing to see. Anything to keep her eyes away from the camera in the log-in screen. In the end Duncan tricked her. He looked behind and shouted, "Look, there it is!" Harriet couldn't help looking and *click* the phone had taken the picture it needed and the screen sprang to life.

It showed a maze of information about Fluffkin: press here to check Fluffkin's well-being, or here for Fluffkin's happiness. His size, his whereabouts, his energy, how long before he needed a recharge all had their own section of the menu. Ursula tried pressing on something called "language development". She half expected to see the word "juice" neatly listed under the word "squeeze", but, in fact, there was a stream of code cascading down the black screen, tiny white letters and numbers that meant nothing. Harriet was obviously enjoying their discomfort. Just as she had predicted, they were much too stupid to understand what they were looking at.

"Zhang would know what it means," said Ursula.

Duncan looked at her. Hearing Ursula speak Zhang's name was to feel this real, flesh and blood world collide with the lovely clean world of Poo-Chi Planet. He suddenly understood that Poo-Chi Planet was really broken, and all the friendships he had made, with Kobe and Zhang and RatboyRyan and the others, they could be broken too.

"Listen," said Ursula, blushing. "I'm really sorry, I don't know where your phone's gone."

"No, no. I found it." He pulled it out of his back pocket and showed her.

She smiled a proper smile, overwhelmed with relief. "I thought I'd lost it."

He flicked it on and there, magically, delightfully, was a message.

Kobe says, "It is me, Kobe, your Poo-Chi friend. Poo-Chi Planet is no more but we, dear friend, are still here. Please send reply for contact."

Somehow Kobe in Kenya had fished out the contact details for all his Poo-Chi friends as the website went down. Duncan and Ursula grinned at each other.

Duncan got busy messaging Kobe, explaining what had happened. Here he was telling another person, half a world away, about marauding monsters, smashed up apartments and a girl wrapped in sticky tape, but Kobe seemed to accept it all. It was a great relief to simply be believed.

Mr Meager asked his daughter, "What's he bothering with that for? How is talking to that lad in Kenya going to help?" She hugged him.

"You're so old-fashioned, Dad."

Kobe explained, using messages to Duncan on his phone, how to divert the stream of code on Harriet's phone and send it to him in Kenya. Duncan and Ursula followed his instructions carefully but there was a horrible moment when everything went black. They were just about to give up when Kobe sent them another message.

Kobe says, "Too much code, crashed. Sent it also to Zhang we both work on."

"Thank you," Duncan messaged back.

After a quick discussion they decided to leave Harriet where she was, trussed up in what was left of her apartment. Ursula still thought the best thing would be to bomb Arthritis Hall to the ground, but Duncan and Mr Meager disagreed.

"We have to warn everybody," said Duncan. "After all, if we knew there was a rampaging rhino or a forklift truck with no driver we'd tell people, wouldn't we?"

"I wouldn't tell Grunter," muttered Ursula, but, in the end, she agreed. So leaving Harriet to shout and complain to no one in particular, they trudged up floor after floor. Duncan held his phone out in front of him, as if to light the way. He was watching for messages from Kobe. Ursula and Mr Meager listened out for the monster, jumping every time they heard a creak of the pipes or the wind whistling through a cracked window.

It was only when they were nearly back at the top floor that Ursula remembered something. She stopped still and extended her arms. "Pork Pie!" she exclaimed. "I forgot about Pork Pie!"

*The monster dropped Crusher in a soggy, broken heap
and picked up the pale young lady receptionist.*

-13-

ALMOST THE END OF EVERYTHING

Perhaps it was a good thing that everybody on the top floor was collected together in the Operations Room. Duncan, Ursula and Mr Meager all had reason to fear the terrible Mrs Grunt but with everyone gathered in one place maybe they could nip in quickly, pass on their warning to someone sensible and then retreat before they were even noticed.

"Ready?" asked Duncan.

Ursula and her father nodded grimly.

As they shuffled in everyone looked up from their papers and stared. Crusher Bacon dug Toffee in the ribs.

"Look! It's that little spy bloke!"

The only one who did not notice the new arrivals, and who would not have cared if she had, was Mrs Pettigrew. She was still slumped in the corner, playing her computer game. She had accumulated a score of 13,714: very close to her personal best. All she had to do was steer her character safely through the Farting Fields of Albion, avoiding the Rodents of Retribution. Then she would have the highest score of anyone on the planet ever.

Mr Meager cleared his throat nervously. "Excuse me, Linoleum, can I have a word?" he began.

"No!" yelled Mrs Grunt. "You can't!" She used her pointer to signal to five of the biggest technicians, who got up and stood around the three newcomers menacingly.

Mr Meager tried again: "Linoleum, I really think—"

"Did I not make myself clear?" shrieked Mrs Grunt, glaring down at the ragged little party. "You can hand over your prisoner when I have dealt with questions." She obviously thought Mr Meager was there to hand over Duncan. Ursula bristled at the idea.

"There's a monster on the loose," she yelled. "It's very dangerous."

"Really? There's a monster on the loose," repeated Mrs Grunt. She dropped the word "monster" like a stone into water. Some of the villains sniggered. The technicians leant in closer.

"Mr Malone," Mrs Grunt turned back to the villains in front of her and spoke with exaggerated evenness, "please repeat your question."

"Can you move the Googley from here?" asked Sharpy Malone.

Mrs Grunt used her pointer to draw his attention to a particular screen showing a very grand interior in St Petersburg, Russia. She tapped one of the technicians smartly on the head. "Demonstrate!" she snapped.

Somewhere inside a palace in that lovely, wintery city, the Googley that the lady ambassador had bought for her small son turned a stately circle for no reason whatsoever. Nobody was there to watch it happen but if they had been, what would they have thought? It's just a child's toy, who worries about a toy? Meanwhile, at the top of Arthritis Hall a selection of villains noted the paintings, furniture and priceless porcelain vases as they slipped past their view. A couple of them gave an appreciative whistle.

"Is that a Van Gogh?" Toffee asked Jago quietly.

"It's seven Van Goghs, old sport. Seven all in one room just begging to be taken on a trip to somewhere more interesting, like a nice bank vault with my name on it. What did I tell you?"

"You have to hand it to her," said Toffee to himself, shaking his head.

"As you can see, GrumpO Industries now has its sources in place." Mrs Grunt tapped a picture of a

Googley with her pointer and glared at the collected villains in front of her, daring them not to understand her. "What we require is teams of opera-teevs who can collect, for a reasonable percentage, what our sources have found for us."

"Linoleum, I really think..." insisted Mr Meager. But, at that moment, the screens switched to show a life-sized bronze elk with raised head and bared teeth that had once stood in General Spoon's billiard room, and nobody was interested in what Mr Meager thought. There were gasps from around the room. The whereabouts of this artwork had been discussed recently in the papers and they were all interested to know how much it was worth.

"I cannot disclose the exact sum," said Mrs Grunt, in her icy little sing-song voice. "But the resale value is in seven figures."

The assembled villains gave a collective sigh of pleasure like dieters biting into a chocolate cake.

Jago started clapping. He stood, gesturing to his fellow villains to also get to their feet and show their appreciation. Most of them obeyed, unsure what was going on but keen not to be left out. The effect was a rather ragged and anxious standing ovation. Jago Lumsden beamed at Mrs Grunt with an expression of deep adoration.

"Brilliant!" he declared. "Sheer brilliance. I take my hat off to you, dear lady, a star in our profession. The idea of getting children to buy a toy that will, effectively, spy on your behalf. Inspired!" He shook his head as if he could hardly believe such a stroke of genius was possible. If you knew where to look there were signs, around the corners of her little pink mouth, that Mrs Grunt was beginning to thaw.

"May I ask a question, dear lady?" Jago smarmed. Mrs Grunt raised one eyebrow. "Can you use this superb system of yours to broadcast speech? Is it possible to talk through it?"

Mrs Grunt tapped a technician smartly on the head again with her pointer.

"Number sixty-seven is live," he muttered.

Screen sixty-seven was the one showing a small girl apparently singing to her Googley. Mrs Grunt took the microphone from the top of the lectern and handed it not to Jago, who had been expecting it, he was not to be forgiven that easily, but to Crusher Bacon sitting next to him.

"What would you like to say, Mr Bacon?" she asked. "Whatever you say into this microphone that child, who is, I believe, in Kerala, India, will hear from the mouth of her new toy."

Crusher was actually tremendously pleased to be asked; it was not often people let him use his own initiative.

"Listen here, girlie," he growled. "If you don't put me down right now I'm going to climb into your bed tonight, drill into your ear, right through your brain, then out the other side." The look of horror on the girl's face as she dropped her Googley made the Operations Room erupt into laughter. Some of the villains slapped Crusher on the back. He blushed with pleasure. Mrs Grunt gave them a few moments to let off steam then she banged her pointer on the lectern to re-establish order.

"That par-tic-u-lar facility will not be used friv-olously," she bawled. "Do I make myself clear?"

"Would serve you right," Ursula shouted, "if Fluffkin killed you all."

"You stupid, noxious, unhygienic infant," bawled Mrs Grunt. "I am not interested in the ridiculous fantasies of your re-volt-ing little mind. You and your appalling father have been a millstone round my neck! Why? Who says I owe you anything? An accident of birth apparently! It may surprise the pair of you, but I have rights as well! If he can't keep you under control I will make sure he loses his job and his home and that you are removed permanently from his care. IS THAT CLEAR?"

There was silence. Many of the villains coughed nervously and looked at their shoes. Mr Meager put an arm round his daughter.

What, Duncan wondered, *did she mean by "an accident of birth"*? It didn't make any sense.

It was then that Duncan's phone buzzed, a new message.

RatboyRyan says, "Are you OK? Got message from Zhang. She and Kobe want to use my computer."

Duncan says, "Yes, seriously please." He was about to type more but...

RatboyRyan says, "Jeez, got visuals now. Jeez, what is this?"

Duncan wanted to explain to RatboyRyan that he had no idea what was happening, if RatboyRyan could find out, could he please explain it to him? He handed his phone to Ursula. "One more try," he whispered.

"Excuse me," he asked the technician next to him. The technician stepped aside. It is actually quite hard not to be polite to someone who is being polite to you. Duncan climbed up next to Mrs Grunt. They stared at each other. Her ears, he noticed, were going a violent shade of pink and it looked as if inside her pink suit her armpits were getting clammy. Duncan turned to face his audience.

"I know this is going to sound a bit weird," he told the delegates. "But—" He didn't get any further than that because the moment the word "but" came out of his mouth something completely unexpected happened: something so bizarre and worrying that it would put an end, for a while, to innocent daydreams, musings, conjecture and personal reflections of any kind.

A missile came shooting straight through the wall of screens high above their heads, bringing with it a shower of bits of wire, glass and plastic. Instinctively they all ducked down but it wasn't an exploding sort of missile, it was more of a pod-shaped package made up of layers and layers of parcel tape. It skidded across the floor and came to a crashing halt, then lay there, howling pitifully.

Ursula came forward. She picked up the package from the ground and delivered it to Duncan. Their eyes met, they were both pretty sure what it contained. While Mrs Grunt, Ursula, Jago, Crusher, the technicians, the pale young lady receptionist and everybody else watched him, Duncan pulled away enough of the tape to see the sour eye and dusty fur inside. He didn't cut away any more. He simply handed the package to Mrs Grunt. As she looked down at what she had been given, a pink flush collected around her knees and rose up through her body. Pork Pie was a broken and defeated cat. A cat with great chunks of fur missing. A cat so shocked and appalled by what had happened to him that he was overwhelmed with self-pity.

Ursula watched with satisfaction as Mrs Grunt went bright pink in the face. *Perhaps she'll have a heart attack*, she thought cheerfully.

"What have you done to Pork Pie?" screamed Mrs Grunt. "What have you done to him?" Her rage was so loud it could be heard beyond our solar system. People covered their ears. She lashed out with her pointer. People covered their heads, which turned out to be a good idea in view of what happened next.

Excited by so much noise and so many little wriggling people, Fluffkin, the thrower of the package, arrived. He exploded straight through the wall of screens, like a crocodile bringing panic to a watering hole, in a fantastic cascade of broken glass.

It was the end of the world, complete disaster. Dust erupted in the Operations Room. Shards of flex and glass and plaster rained down. Some people gawped, some screamed, some whimpered. Fluffkin, half frightened, half excited by the noise and panic, whipped his arms around his head and brought them crashing down. He reared up on his back legs, looming over the Operations Room, a tornado of pure fury. Furniture was smashed, equipment went flying, cables fried, computers toppled; it was a riot of destruction. Fluffkin drove his three-pronged hand through desks, sending the sobbing technicians hiding underneath scuttling for safety: little wriggling things, noisy things, smelling of fear.

"Blimey," breathed Mr Meager. He looked around for Ursula. She had grabbed a chair and was holding it up to the monster.

"Come on," she threatened. "I'm not scared of you."

Mrs Grunt had gone chalk white.

RatboyRyan, in Australia, stared, open-mouthed, at his screen. Was it possible that he was watching a disaster that was happening for real? Over the course of his young life he had seen many disasters, so many carefully crafted apocalypses in the various games he played on his computers, but this was different. This was just chaos.

Duncan kept his head. He had an idea that if he could get everyone together they would be safer; harder for the monster to grab a whole group of people than pick them off one by one. It already had Crusher Bacon by the ankles and was bouncing him about in mid-air. Poor Crusher, he was trying not to be sick and was crying for his mum.

"This way," Duncan yelled. Mr Meager grabbed Ursula's hand and hauled her towards Duncan. They crouched behind the lectern together.

The monster dropped Crusher in a soggy, broken heap and picked up the pale young lady receptionist, shaking her up and down experimentally.

"Linoleum," called Mr Meager, holding out his hand to her.

Mrs Grunt seemed frozen. She stared at Mr Meager.

"It's your fault," she shrieked. It was a ridiculous thing to say, of course, but bad people in chaotic situations are not always very fair.

The monster whipped his free arms around the room. One caught Sharpy Malone flat across the stomach and carried him to the far wall.

Sharpy said, "Ohh", then he didn't say anything else.

Kobe says, "Turn to right now."

What? Turn what to the right? In Australia, RatboyRyan picked up his controller and pressed the "turn right" button, and the picture on his screen made a sickening dive down to the ground.

Zhang says, "Correction, try now."

This time the picture followed his instruction and turned right.

"Brilliant!" yelled RatboyRyan, to no one in particular.

Who knows how Zhang and Kobe had taken all that code Duncan had sent from Harriet's phone and turned it into something useful? Something that RatboyRyan could use to control where Fluffkin was looking and see what Fluffkin could see. But that is exactly what they had done!

It turned out that Fluffkin was looking at a grey,

jumbled chaos of broken furniture, upturned computers, dust, broken plaster, wiring and people, all staring up at him, horrified by what they saw.

"Dear lady." The Honourable Jago Lumsden bowed to Mrs Grunt so avoiding the arm slicing through the air where his head had just been. "My private helicopter is still on the roof awaiting my return. If I could be of any assistance to you?" He offered her his arm. He was dusty, and his hair was sticking up, but otherwise he was the same elegant villain, and he was giving her a way out.

"I'll come with you, mate," offered Toffee on his hands and knees under a table.

"Sorry, chum, only room for two." Jago put his expensive, handmade shoe on Toffee's face and shoved him away. Then Jago and Mrs Grunt set off through the debris at a sort of crouching run. Most people didn't notice them go but Ursula did. She flew at Mrs Grunt and grabbed her around the ankle.

"Get off," shrieked Mrs Grunt, kicking out viciously. Ursula hung on. Mrs Grunt dragged her some distance through the dust. Still Ursula would not let go.

"Allow me," said Jago and whacked Ursula hard with a piece of table leg. In the end Mrs Grunt escaped by leaving one bright pink high-heeled shoe in Ursula's arms. She hobbled off with Jago, stopping only to scoop up Pork Pie the cat. It was Toffee, carrying his table on his back like a giant tortoise, who crawled over to rescue Ursula from where she lay, tear-stained and raging in the dust.

Casey J held the Googley up to the mic. She made the musicians and security people be quiet so everyone could hear.

-14-

A DANCE, A DEATH AND SOME
IMPORTANT INFORMATION

"I WILL NOT HAVE THIS NOISE!" screamed Mrs Pettigrew. Everyone stopped. They had forgotten she was there. Which noise did she mean? It might have been Ursula sobbing, or Duncan and Mr Meager calling encouragement to her. Maybe it was the computer Fluffkin had just thrown at the far wall. Whatever it was, Mrs Pettigrew had finally registered that all was not as it should be in the world around her. The interruption came just as her score reached 13,840, breaking her concentration and causing her to make a mistake. She was furious.

"I WON'T HAVE IT!!" Oblivious to the huge monster towering over her, she stamped her foot with each word like an outraged infant. She stamped so hard her football socks escaped her knobbly knees and descended towards her bony ankles.

The frayed circuits in Fluffkin's brain registered this noisy, stampy thing.

What's he going to do? thought Duncan. *He's going to do something.*

If you knew what to look for you would have noticed a terrible battle taking place in Fluffkin's head. It seemed to judder and spasm.

RatboyRyan, suddenly aware of the danger, was trying to haul Fluffkin's gaze away from Mrs Pettigrew. *Look right!* He desperately whacked the button on his controller, *look up, look away.*

Fluffkin tried turning his head to compensate for the fact he no longer seemed able to control where he was looking. It was almost comic the way his head flapped back and forth while his eyes rolled left and right.

"Juice?" demanded Fluffkin in a kind of panic, outraged at the intrusion in his head. "Squeeze, squeeze, squeeze."

Duncan peered over the lectern. "Mrs Pettigrew," he called, trying to draw her attention to the danger.

"YOU AGAIN!" she complained as if Duncan had been pestering her constantly. She was still completely unaware of the monster looming over her. It was difficult to know where to start.

"Be careful," he advised. Which works well as advice in almost every situation, but considering that the monster was eyeing Mrs Pettigrew, and drawing itself up to its full height, you could say it did not go far enough.

RatboyRyan did everything he could to distract Fluffkin. He kept his finger down on the "look right" button, then snapped back the other way for a second. Fluffkin, feeling as if he had wasps in his brain, lifted his head up and looked at the ceiling. What was he doing? Maybe he was listening. Fluffkin became a crocodile, a black-hearted killer listening for his prey.

"WHAT?" screamed Mrs Pettigrew. "SPEAK CLEARLY, BOY."

Fluffkin snapped his jaws. A crocodile can move with great agility when it wants. He opened his mouth, bent down and swallowed her whole. One bite and she was gone.

"It ate her," breathed Toffee, appalled.

"Blimey," added Mr Meager.

The screens that were being used for messaging between Nairobi, Shanghai, Melbourne and Arthritis Hall all went momentarily black, which gave OboCurlyTops a chance to ask an important question.

OboCurlyTops says, "What, what happened?"

RatboyRyan says, "Jeez, sorry, I'm sorry. I couldn't stop

him." RatboyRyan was not used to real consequences and he was shocked.

Zhang says, "Not your fault."

RatboyRyan says, "Sorry mate."

Kobe says, "Need more time."

Zhang says, "Yes need more."

OboCurlyTops says, "What does it want? Does it want juice?"

Zhang says, "Ask it. Juice or what?"

Ursula and Duncan, crouching together behind the lectern, saw the messages flash across the screen of Duncan's phone. OboCurlyTops and Zhang were suggesting that a chat with Fluffkin might buy them time.

"We could try, I suppose," said Duncan.

Ursula shrugged. "Give it a go."

"Perhaps if he's just eaten one person he won't want another for a while."

"Maybe he'll feel full up." They almost smiled at each other but, thinking of what had just happened to Mrs Pettigrew, they stopped themselves.

"We'll take it slowly."

"All right, bossy boots."

Carefully, slowly, Ursula got up onto the box Mrs Grunt had used to make her speech. Slowly, carefully, Duncan climbed up beside her. Mr Meager hissed at his daughter to get back down but she ignored him. Fluffkin eyed them both, suspiciously.

On the lectern in front of them were two things. One was the microphone Crusher Bacon had used to scare the young girl singing to her Googley, the other was Mrs Grunt's pointer. There they were, quietly waiting to be useful.

Ursula picked up the pointer and held it out towards the monster. She had to hold it with both hands to stop it shaking. It was no protection of course, it was a matchstick that the monster could snap at any moment, but still it made her feel braver. RatboyRyan hauled Fluffkin's gaze round so that he couldn't help but look at her.

"Does this microphone work?" Duncan asked the technicians out of the corner of his mouth. Now that the pieces of this absurd puzzle were starting to arrange themselves in his head it seemed to Duncan that warnings needed to go out beyond Arthritis Hall. The whole world needed to be warned.

There was a hushed but urgent discussion, then one of the technicians hissed, "Keep it busy", and crawled off on his hands and knees to try and find a keyboard that was still intact.

How do you keep a monster busy?

"Hey, fatty!" yelled Ursula. "You want some juice?"

That turned out not to be the best approach. Fluffkin picked up a chair and threw it. His aim was good and it broke into pieces on the corner of the lectern. Ursula and Duncan ducked as the fragments flew over their heads.

"All right, calm down, mate," urged RatboyRyan in his bedroom in Australia. "No need for that."

Once all was clear Duncan stood up straight. He steadied himself.

"I was wondering, could we get you something?" His polite, reasonable tone was rather shocking.

"Bet you want some juice, don't you?" asked Ursula.

"Juice?" repeated Fluffkin.

"Not that stupid electric juice, bet you've had enough of that for a while. You can get other kinds you know, apple juice, or Brussels sprout juice, or you can get dead donkey juice, or dead donkey juice with spiders and ham." Fluffkin stared at Ursula. Even if RatboyRyan had not been holding his attention in one place he still would have watched her. When space aliens finally land on our planet and begin explaining, through the medium of dance, how time and space warp each other, we will all probably feel like Fluffkin felt as he watched Ursula: completely baffled but really interested.

OboCurlyTops says, "Dingbat pie flavour, snake eyes plus sherbert dab."

"You want dingbat pie flavour?" Ursula asked Fluffkin.

"Juice?" he replied.

"You want snake eye-juice? You want up, down and sideways juice? You want lemon meringue and hard cheese pieces? You want old man jam and roly-poly steaming dumpling juice with sweaty socks?"

With OboCurlyTops contributing the odd suggestion, Ursula kept up her stream of nonsense.

Every now and then Fluffkin said, "Juice?" just to show he knew how to have a conversation even if he had no idea what this one was about.

"It's a game," Ursula called to him. "You can play. Like bicycle juice. Think of something, make it juice. Old fart and cauliflower juice, everything squished up and mashed together in a slipper juice... You play."

"Play?" said Fluffkin.

"That's it, play," said Ursula. "You say juice juice, like the juice of juice."

"Play?" repeated Fluffkin.

Zhang says, "Try left side now."

The three legs on Fluffkin's left side seemed to give themselves a little shake. Zhang and Kobe had been working furiously and they thought they had the code that controlled that set of legs. Now RatboyRyan could take over. He made a kind of scooping motion with his controller and carefully eased the three legs up and around and back down to the ground. His heart, he realised, was pounding.

Kobe had an idea.

Kobe says, "Dance. It maybe help read code faster."

OboCurlyTops says, "Get him to dance."

"Hey!" called Ursula. She drew a figure of eight above her head with the tip of the pointer. While Fluffkin watched she kept it moving, making big sweeping movements. At the same time she started to dance. It wasn't much of a dance; all it involved was hopping from foot to foot, but it turned out to be exactly what was required. As Ursula hopped lumpily around, RatboyRyan used the controller to lift up Fluffkin's left legs in imitation. Then, miraculously, Zhang and Kobe watched the code change as Fluffkin himself tried to move his right side.

That's it, Fluffkin! Watch Ursula, copy her.

"How many channels you want open?" the technician whispered to Duncan.

Repeated movement, that was the thing. Movement Fluffkin could copy. RatboyRyan got Fluffkin to sway from side to side and jig from one set of legs to the other. Zhang in China and Kobe in Kenya watched the code ebb and flow; finally they could see how Fluffkin worked.

"Diddle diddle dum dum," chanted Ursula in time with her slow plodding dance. "Kiss my bum... Don't eat me... Eat my mum."

Duncan was a little bit shocked by this. Why was she suddenly talking about her mother? She had never mentioned a mother before.

Kobe says, "Try now."

RatboyRyan swung the controller, pulling up, then setting down Fluffkin's right legs.

Yes, they had control of some of his movement.

Ursula turned a slow and majestic circle.

Do the same, Fluffkin, try and do the same. There were one or two moments when all Fluffkin's limbs seemed to freeze at once, but slowly, clumsily, RatboyRyan led Fluffkin round in a matching circle.

"Laddie," hissed the technician. "I'm not down here for the good of my health! How many channels?"

A computer went flying an inch above his head and smashed spectacularly against the back wall. RatboyRyan might be in control of Fluffkin's legs but he didn't yet have control of all of him. *Keep working, Zhang and Kobe.*

"Every channel," Duncan told the technician. Ursula carried on her plodding dance, hopping like a baby elephant from foot to foot, waving the pointer and turning slow stately circles.

"Diddle diddle dum dum... Kiss my bum... Don't eat me... Eat my mum."

"Why should he eat your mum?" Duncan asked her out of the corner of his mouth.

"So she doesn't get away with greasy old Jago."

Duncan was stunned.

"Mrs Grunt is your mother?" He could not believe it. "I thought you hated her."

"I do."

"You're live," the technician hissed.

Ursula was Mrs Grunt's daughter! Duncan thought he had never heard anything so ridiculous in his whole life.

"Laddie, will you stop dreaming!"

What would you say if you knew your voice was going to come out of the mouths of all of the thirty million Googleys that had been sold around the world? Duncan collected himself, there was a lot of explaining to do.

The President of the United States was being driven through Washington in the back of a long black car with black windows. There was a security guard on one side of her and a Googley on the other. The Googley had been given to her by her grandson so she would have someone nice to talk to.

"This is your Googley speaking," said the Googley in Duncan's voice. "And here is the Googley news. Your Googley is looking at you now, it's watching everything you do."

The security guard reached over and shot the Googley in the head. The President tutted and brushed bits of orange fluff off her jacket.

There goes my last chance for a sensible conversation, she thought.

The arena was full of screaming fans. Casey J should have been on stage five minutes ago. What Casey would have liked to be doing was playing a nice game of Scrabble with her nan. She stuck her finger up her nose and had a good root around. How come everybody else except her got to stay home and play Scrabble with their nan? It wasn't fair.

Her Googley, sitting on her dressing table, suddenly started talking: "Here are the Googley headlines. Your Googley is watching you. It can see everything you do."

Casey took her finger out of her nose. Duncan went on to explain how Googleys had been designed to spy for crooks and villains, kidnappers, blackmailers, forgers and thieves.

All around the world all the Googleys were saying the same thing at the same time. At international airports the same voice came from Googleys shut in suitcases. Googleys arranged on shelves explained how Googleys could see log-in details and passwords and security codes because no one thought to hide that sort of thing from a toy.

"Seriously, shut up and listen." Casey J had taken her Googley on to the stage. She held it up to the mic and yelled at the musicians and security people to be quiet so that everyone in the stadium could hear.

"Googleys can see where your mum keeps her jewellery, where Dad keeps the keys to his car." A couple of thousand eleven-year-old girls in the arena also considered that their Googleys had probably heard what they had said about their teacher, their sister, their best friend. By the time Duncan started to talk about the particular problems they were having in Arthritis Hall most people had stopped listening.

Googleys were shut in cupboards, pushed under beds or turned to the wall.

"I think I've changed my mind," said a mother to the sales assistant in Jerrard's toy department, handing back the Googley she had been about to buy. Displays disappeared from shops. Consignments in mid-air lost all their value, while lawyers eagerly wondered who might sue whom.

In a cottage near Arthritis Hall, Trumpy the dog dragged a still-talking Googley into the front room where Police Constable Brian Kerr had just got in from a long shift and was taking off his boots. Brian listened to Duncan describe what was going on at Arthritis Hall. He didn't believe a word of it but he sighed and put his boots back on anyway. Trumpy wagged his tail. He was a dog that loved to fight crime.

Meanwhile, a small theatre in San Francisco was about to put on a production called "Googleys do the Sound of Music". Sixty-eight Googleys, dressed in little nuns' costumes, were arranged on stage. They suddenly all shouted in Duncan's voice, "Look out, Ursula!"

The monster had reached down and picked her up. It was not something RatboyRyan had made him do, Fluffkin simply seemed to want a closer look. Mr Meager, Toffee Cheeseman and Duncan were all yelling for Fluffkin to be careful. Ursula, trembling with fear,

clapped a hand across her mouth to stop herself showing it. RatboyRyan tried to turn Fluffkin to stop him
picking up anybody else but things went a bit wrong
and the monster actually tripped over his own legs
and fell. Ursula disappeared under those huge grinding
metal plates.

They all held their breath.

"Better not hurt her," whispered RatboyRyan. He
was listening really hard. Somehow he could feel the
fizzing in Fluffkin's brain through his fingers. *He's
frightened and he doesn't get why they're shouting. He wants
to get away.*

If this had been a computer game, RatboyRyan would
simply have to decide on the direction and off they
would have charged, but this was different, this was
almost the opposite of playing a computer game. It was
beginning to dawn on RatboyRyan, Kobe, Duncan and
Zhang that having control over the code that governed
most of Fluffkin's many limbs was not the same as
having control over him.

Mr Meager tugged desperately at Duncan's sleeve.
"Please do something, son."

Duncan tried to look encouraging. "Honestly, we're
trying."

"Steady, mate," RatboyRyan urged Fluffkin. "It's OK,
we can do this." He tried to soothe the fizzing wires of
Fluffkin's brain with his own slowness and coolness.
"All right, no worries!"

Zhang had isolated the code governing the arm that held Ursula and she flicked it halfway around the world to RatboyRyan's bedroom in Melbourne. Slowly, gently, he curled Fluffkin's arm against his body.

Ursula tried not to shriek, she thought she was going to be crushed, but no, Fluffkin stopped in time. Holding her carefully, even tenderly.

RatboyRyan says, "He wants to get away."

Zhang says, "Can you stop him?"

RatboyRyan says, "Don't know, maybe, but will be fight with him."

Kobe says, "Fight bad for Ursula."

OboCurlyTops says, "Let him go."

Duncan says, "Let him run but protect her."

"Right," RatboyRyan said to himself as well as to Fluffkin, "we're going to keep this slow and calm." He needed to send one more message.

RatboyRyan says, "Watch out, guys."

Sometimes the best thing to do is nothing. What RatboyRyan didn't do, and this was a little bit of genius that could have gone completely unnoticed, he didn't try and make Fluffkin do anything. He held his breath and kept his hands still.

"You're in charge, mate, but I'm coming with you," he told Fluffkin.

Slowly, hesitantly, Fluffkin began to untangle his own legs.

-15-

THE BATTLE OF ARTHRITIS HALL

S TILL HOLDING URSULA, Fluffkin turned and charged out of the Operations Room. Suddenly RatboyRyan was riding an organic robot the size of a school bus as it burst through walls and tore open rooms. Fluffkin was not yet used to his new size and he didn't know where his edges were. Doorways shattered and walls crumbled as he simply drove through them, leaving brickwork, woodwork, silver trees, white button chairs and marble fountains utterly broken in his wake. Imagine how start-led Nathan felt as the door to the caretaker's cupboard burst open and a huge three-pronged metal hand reached in, scattering the mops. It is not nice to say, now that he is such a big star, but I believe he wet himself.

Fluffkin didn't know where he was going, he just knew he wanted to get away. Duncan and Toffee and Mr Meager all streamed after him, shouting that he should think about Ursula. Fluffkin wanted to hold her out ahead of him, like a figurehead on a ship, but RatboyRyan kept control of the arm holding her, making it dodge left then right, up then down as Fluffkin ploughed through the next lot of masonry. At some point between the smashed reception desk and exploding cloakrooms, RatboyRyan relaxed and began to enjoy himself. *Wow, what a ride.*

Above all the shouting and yelling, Fluffkin could hear something new. A juddering, rhythmic buzzing, as if there was a giant insect somewhere close. He knew what to do with buzzing things. Stairs led up to the roof and the door at the top was open, showing a small but inviting rectangle of blue sky.

"What's he going to do now?" shouted Ursula in a panic. "He'll never fit through there." What he did was erupt, headfirst, straight through the roof. She squeezed her eyes shut and balled her fists, bracing for the impact. It never came. Bricks and masonry and tiles cascaded down around her but RatboyRyan, in Melbourne, kept her safe. Duncan and Toffee and Mr Meager followed them up using what was left of the stairs. Up they went, bursting on to the roof, blinded by sunshine, sucking in clean air. And there was Ursula, held up like a torch, dusty and spluttering. She raised her hand to show she was OK, in fact, she realised, she was more than OK.

Mrs Linoleum Grunt and the Honourable Jago Lumsden were strapped into the front seats of his helicopter; the engines were firing, the blades were turning and the sky was clear. What did they think as Fluffkin reared up, gleaming and huge, waving five of his arms and dangling Ursula in front of them with the other?

Mrs Grunt went very pale, her mouth fell open, but it was probably not because she was thinking about the danger her dear daughter was in.

Duncan found himself next to Mr Meager. They both kept their gaze fixed on Ursula, as if by staring they could keep her safe.

"So she's her mother?" Duncan asked. This still seemed to him the most bizarre idea.

Mr Meager nodded.

"They don't get on very well, do they?" suggested Duncan.

"Nope," he agreed. "Too alike I sometimes think. Linoleum's very ambitious you see. Always got some scheme or other."

Duncan did not reply to this. In his opinion Ursula was nothing like her terrible mother.

"Step on it!" Mrs Grunt was shouting at Jago, who was so astonished by the sight of Ursula he had forgotten to move.

"Stop them getting away," Ursula shouted, not entirely sure who she was shouting at. Maybe RatboyRyan, maybe Fluffkin, maybe Duncan and her father, maybe Zhang and Kobe and the twins in Texas. Since she was dangling in front of the windscreen, she took the chance to stick her tongue out at her mother. Mrs Grunt went white with fury, then purpley pink, then liver coloured; she screamed, she snarled and ground her teeth. Ursula watched her mother perform a silent pantomime of rage. Her big pink face suddenly looked ridiculous.

"Come on, mate, let's do this right," urged RatboyRyan somewhere inside Fluffkin's head. "First thing's first."

He tried to turn the arm holding Ursula and Fluffkin took the hint. He placed her carefully down next to her very relieved father. Fluffkin had bigger fish to fry.

The helicopter lifted off, and RatboyRyan could feel the excitement fizzing through Fluffkin's circuits.

"Catch them," shouted Duncan.

"We can do it!" RatboyRyan told Fluffkin. He collected himself in his bedroom in Melbourne. Fluffkin collected himself on top of Arthritis Hall.

The helicopter rose upwards.

"Now or never!"

They gathered all their strength, tensing every muscle. "Now!"

Fluffkin leapt up and out. RatboyRyan roared so hard he woke his parents in the next room. Fluffkin's three-pronged hand scraped then grabbed on to the undercarriage of the helicopter. He got another hand fixed on to the giant buzzing thing, then another and another. The helicopter nearly crashed with the sudden added weight but Jago fought for control and was just about able to pull clear of the building.

Police Constable Brian Kerr, on his bicycle, rode between the lines of greasy black pine trees that surrounded Arthritis Hall with Trumpy the dog in the basket at the front. Brian was thinking about his dinner, sausages and mash, and jam roly-poly for afters, all now spoiling in the oven while he was on this wild goose chase. It was Trumpy who looked up and saw what was happening.

What a battle was going on in the sky above their heads! With a huge, monstrous robotic creature hanging from its undercarriage, the helicopter could not get enough height to escape. It fell towards the ground, then pulled away only to fall again. The chaos that must have been going on in the cockpit can only be imagined, what with Mrs Linoleum Grunt shouting and Pork Pie scratching and Jago snarling. Fluffkin, meanwhile, was busy trying to wrap the biggest fly he had ever seen.

As the helicopter lurched along above Herbert's Bottom, people stopped their cars. They came out into playgrounds and gardens to look up and take photographs. How long do you imagine it took before they knew all about the battle of Arthritis Hall on the other side of the world: ten minutes? Five? Two?

Duncan, Toffee, Ursula and Mr Meager had heard Trumpy bark and seen Constable Kerr get on his radio but they stayed on the roof watching the helicopter get smaller and smaller as it juddered towards the horizon.

"Blimey," repeated Mr Meager several times, his arm around his daughter.

Toffee gave Duncan a shove.

"You're a sharp one, aren't you?" he said approvingly. "Fooled us!" He smiled at Duncan and Duncan smiled back.

Then Duncan took Ursula's hand and lifted it in the air. He wanted to say something like, "We did it!" But when you have just saved yourself and everybody else from a giant organic robot while at the same time foiling plans to steal from millions of families around the world, it's hard to find the right words.

"Wow! That's a relief" was about the best he could do. It was only now that he could stop being frightened that he realised how very frightened he had been.

Ursula nodded. "Blimey!" she said, grinning.

There was a message on the phone:

Zhang, Kobe, RatboyRyan, OboCurlyTops say, "BRILLIANT BRILLIANT YOU ARE WORLD CHAMPIONS AND SO ARE WE!"

Then Ursula started to do a dance; at least, she started to stamp up and down and toss her head from side to side and fling her arms about and whoop.

Rumour has it that Fluffkin was finally forced to land at a military airfield by Air Force jets, the helicopter still firmly in his grip. He was, apparently, accommodated in an aircraft hangar until Great Aunt Harriet could be fetched. You may even have heard that she was collected, still attached to the tuba, by two gentlemen from The Secret Service who had an offer of work for her from the government. An offer she was not allowed to refuse. However, we should not discuss that any further because when military intelligence get involved things can get a bit cloudy.

It may be that the same Secret Service knows what happened to Mrs Grunt. She is probably stuck in a damp bungalow on a distant island with only Jago and Pork Pie for company. The heat must be a trial to all three of them. So must their diet of tinned mackerel. I expect they spend all day bickering with each other, dreaming of the impossible: escape.

It wasn't long before the new improved Poo-Chi Planet was launched and of course everybody, including

Ursula, became members. Poo-Chi pets worked with the sort of steady determination their operators never showed for their schoolwork to build up big scores, rise through the levels and fill their apartments with every kind of trophy Poo-Chi Planet had to offer. RatboyRyan still sometimes bought himself a Poo-Chi Planet popsicle and chatted with the others at the Poo-Chi Planet ice rink, but because he had to be the best at every single computer game he didn't have a lot of time to spare. Zhang and Kobe were also busy with other things. You would think the world would have noticed how clever they were but in fact nobody seemed very interested. That is until twelve years exactly from the day this story ends when they revealed their new invention. It was so amazing, so spectacular, that nothing in the world was ever quite the same again. OboCurlyTops in Texas lost interest in Poo-Chi Planet. The twins tried cheerleading, then chess, then being a bobsleigh team, then découpage (which means sticking pictures of things on things). Then bareback riding, then stamp collecting. Every new hobby offered new opportunities to disagree.

You have probably also heard how Duncan's mum and dad were so grateful to Mr Meager for looking after

Duncan while they were in Japan that they used all their many contacts to find him a new job. It came with a little house and a garden for him to share with his daughter. Duncan's parents even built them a tree house. If there are any adults reading this story they would probably like to imagine Duncan and Ursula scampering among the foliage, playing pirates, making pirate noises and waving pretend cutlasses about. Of course this is not what they actually did. They actually used the tree house to climb up where their parents could not see them and sit side by side playing new improved Poo-Chi Planet on their phones. Duncan built the best Poo-Chi apartment anyone has ever seen while Ursula preferred to hang about at the ice rink arguing with Kobe and Zhang and RatboyRyan and anyone else that happened by.

Nathan was soon on every television show explaining how he saved the world from the evil Mrs Grunt. Meanwhile, Crusher married his lady love in a grand ceremony attended by every villain and crook in the city but his new wife would not let him try the chocolate fountain in case he got fat. That just leaves Toffee. I'm sure you don't need me to tell you how he gave up a life of crime and went to work in the little wool shop

"Wow! That's a relief" was about the best Duncan could
do. It was only now that he could stop being frightened
that he realised how very frightened he had been.
Ursula nodded. "Blimey!" she said, grinning.

PUSHKIN CHILDREN'S BOOKS

We created Pushkin Children's Books to share tales from different languages and cultures with younger readers, and to open the door to the wide, colourful worlds these stories offer.

From picture books and adventure stories to fairy tales and classics, and from fifty-year-old bestsellers to current huge successes abroad, the books on the Pushkin Children's list reflect the very best stories from around the world, for our most discerning readers of all: children.

THE BEGINNING WOODS

MALCOLM MCNEILL

'I loved every word and was envious of quite a few... A
modern classic. Rich, funny and terrifying'
Eoin Colfer

THE RED ABBEY CHRONICLES

MARIA TURTSCHANINOFF

1 · *Maresi*
2 · *Naondel*

'Embued with myth, wonder, and told with
a dazzling, compelling ferocity'
Kiran Millwood Hargrave, author of *The Girl of Ink and Stars*

THE LETTER FOR THE KING

TONKE DRAGT

'*The Letter for the King* will get pulses racing... Pushkin
Press deserves every praise for publishing this beautifully
translated, well-presented and captivating book'
The Times

THE SECRETS OF THE WILD WOOD

TONKE DRAGT

'Offers intrigue, action and escapism'
Sunday Times

THE SONG OF SEVEN

TONKE DRAGT

'A cracking adventure... so nail-biting you'll need to wear protective gloves'
The Times

THE MURDERER'S APE

JAKOB WEGELIUS

'A thrilling adventure. Prepare to meet the remarkable
Sally Jones; you won't soon forget her'
Publishers Weekly

THE PARENT TRAP · THE FLYING CLASSROOM · DOT AND ANTON

ERICH KÄSTNER

Illustrated by Walter Trier

'The bold line drawings by Walter Trier are the work of genius... As for the stories, if you're a fan of *Emil and the Detectives*, then you'll find these just as spirited'

Spectator

FROM THE MIXED-UP FILES OF MRS. BASIL E. FRANKWEILER

E. L. KONIGSBURG

'Delightful... I love this book... a beautifully written adventure, with endearing characters and full of dry wit, imagination and inspirational confidence'

Daily Mail

THE RECKLESS SERIES

CORNELIA FUNKE

1 · *The Petrified Flesh*
2 · *Living Shadows*
3 · *The Golden Yarn*

'A wonderful storyteller'

Sunday Times

THE WILDWITCH SERIES

LENE KAABERBØL

1 · *Wildfire*
2 · *Oblivion*
3 · *Life Stealer*
4 · *Bloodling*

'Classic fantasy adventure... Young readers will be delighted to hear that there are more adventures to come for Clara'

Lovereading

MEET AT THE ARK AT EIGHT!

ULRICH HUB

Illustrated by Jörg Mühle

'Of all the books about a penguin in a suitcase pretending to be God asking for a cheesecake, this one is absolutely, definitely my favourite'

Independent

THE SNOW QUEEN

HANS CHRISTIAN ANDERSEN

Illustrated by Lucie Arnoux

'A lovely edition [of a] timeless story'
The Lady

THE WILD SWANS

HANS CHRISTIAN ANDERSEN

'A fresh new translation of these two classic fairy tales recreates the
lyrical beauty and pathos of the Danish genius' evergreen stories'
The Bay

THE CAT WHO CAME IN OFF THE ROOF

ANNIE M.G. SCHMIDT

'Guaranteed to make anyone 7-plus to 107 who likes to
curl up with a book and a cat purr with pleasure'
The Times

LAFCADIO: THE LION WHO SHOT BACK

SHEL SILVERSTEIN

'A story which is really funny, yet also teaches us a great
deal about what we want, what we think we want and what
we are no longer certain about once we have it'
Irish Times

THE SECRET OF THE BLUE GLASS

TOMIKO INUI

'I love this book... How important it is, in these times, that our children
read the stories from other peoples, other cultures, other times'
Michael Morpurgo, *Guardian*

THE STORY OF THE BLUE PLANET

ANDRI SNÆR MAGNASON

Illustrated by Áslaug Jónsdóttir

'A Seussian mix of wonder, wit and gravitas'
The New York Times

THE WITCH IN THE BROOM CUPBOARD AND OTHER TALES

PIERRE GRIPARI

Illustrated by Fernando Puig Rosado

'Wonderful... funny, tender and daft'
David Almond

CLEMENTINE LOVES RED

KRYSTYNA BOGLAR

'A dizzying dance'
Ricochet Jeunes

SHOLA AND THE LIONS

BERNARDO ATXAGA

Illustrated by Mikel Valverde

'Gently ironic stories... totally charming'
Independent

PIGLETTES

CLEMENTINE BEAUVAIS

'A jubilant novel that will make you smile. A true joy'
Le Monde

SAVE THE STORY

GULLIVER · ANTIGONE · CAPTAIN NEMO · DON JUAN
GILGAMESH · THE BETROTHED · THE NOSE
CYRANO DE BERGERAC · KING LEAR · CRIME AND PUNISHMENT

'An amazing new series from Pushkin Press in which literary, adult authors
retell classics (with terrific illustrations) for a younger generation'
Daily Telegraph

THE OKSA POLLOCK SERIES

ANNE PLICHOTA AND CENDRINE WOLF

1 · *The Last Hope*
2 · *The Forest of Lost Souls*
3 · *The Heart of Two Worlds*
4 · *Tainted Bonds*

'A feisty heroine, lots of sparky tricks and evil opponents could
fill a gap left by the end of the Harry Potter series'
Daily Mail